"*Vernon Downs* belongs to a tradition that includes Nicholson Baker's *U and I*, Geoff Dyer's *Out of Sheer Rage*, and—for that matter—*Pale Fire*. What makes Clarke's excellent novel stand out isn't just its rueful intelligence, or its playful semi-veiling of certain notorious literary figures, but its startling sadness. *Vernon Downs* is first rate."

—MATTHEW SPECKTOR, author of *American Dream Machine*

"Moving and edgy in just the right way. Love (or lack of) and Family (or lack of) is at the heart of this wonderfully obsessive novel."

—GARY SHTEYNGART, author of *Super Sad True Love Story*

"*Vernon Downs* is a brilliant meditation on obsession, art, and celebrity. Charlie Marten's mounting fixation with the titular Vernon is not only driven by the burn of heartbreak, but also a lost young man's struggle to locate his place in the world. *Vernon Downs* is an intoxicating novel, and Clarke is a dazzling literary talent."

—LAURA VAN DEN BERG, author of *The Isle of Youth*

"An engrossing novel about longing and impersonation, which is to say, a story about the distance between persons, distances within ourselves. Clarke's prose is infused with music and intelligence and deep feeling."

—CHARLES YU, author of *Sorry Please Thank You*

"*Vernon Downs* is a fascinating and sly tribute to a certain fascinating and sly writer, but this novel also perfectly captures the lonely distortions of a true obsession."

—DANA SPIOTTA, author of *Stone Arabia*

Vernon Downs

Vernon Downs

A NOVEL

Jaime Clarke

Roundabout Press   2014

Published by
Roundabout Press
PO Box 370310
West Hartford, CT 06137

10   9   8   7   6   5   4   3   2   1

FIRST EDITION

For my mother and father

and in memory of Liam Rector

It was only now clear to me how very much I had made that image, and yet I could not feel that it was anything like a fiction. It was more like a special sort of truth, almost a touchstone; as if a thought of mine could become a thing, and at the same time be truth.

—Iris Murdoch, *The Sea, The Sea*

Vernon Downs

I

CHARLIE HAD TRAVELED a long, indirect route to Summit Terrace. He could hardly recall a time he hadn't known the name Vernon Downs, though in truth the discovery was in the not-too-distant past.

"He's Olivia's favorite writer, dummy," Shelleyan had said that day in the Milky Way Café at Glendale Community College, where Charlie and Olivia were creative writing majors. It was his second stint at GCC; he knew from his first stab, after graduating from high school, that even though he was pushing thirty, he wasn't the oldest student on campus. That Olivia was twenty-two separated her—and him—from the student body full of teenagers who mostly behaved like they were still in high school, and the retirees taking classes as a hobby. Only Shelleyan could make him self-conscious of his advanced age. He ignored her, long used to Olivia's roommate as the price of Olivia's companionship. He'd met Olivia, an international student from London, the previous semester in Intro to Creative Writing. Over the prior summer, Charlie had read an interview with a writer who had a background similar to his—the writer was an army brat and had lived all over the world—and how that sense of impermanence informed his writing. Whether or not the writer was being self-deprecating, Charlie couldn't tell, but the piece spooked him a little, as the writer seemed to intimate that there was no place in the workaday world for those with such an upbringing. And so he enrolled in the creative writing class with more hope than ambition.

Discovering Olivia across the conference table seemed to confirm the impression Charlie had taken away from the interview. Olivia's nationality gave her an air of otherness, and Charlie perceived a kinship in the way she was both present but from somewhere else entirely. Olivia hadn't told her parents that she'd dropped out of Arizona State University the first week of the fall semester so she could pocket the difference in tuition between ASU and GCC. If anyone could fully comprehend the narrative of his past and, more importantly, overlook its irregularities, it was Olivia, who confessed that she liked the attention, which was all the encouragement Charlie needed. What began as a crush on a pretty girl with a sexy accent quickly evolved.

"What did he write?" Charlie asked Shelleyan, the name Vernon Downs vaguely familiar. He glanced at Olivia as she combed through that day's goulash with her fork.

"*Minus Numbers*," Shelleyan answered automatically, scooping a forkful into her mouth.

He looked at Olivia for help, but she was apparently absorbed in thoughts of Vernon Downs and *Minus Numbers*. More troubling than the notion of Olivia's secret admiration was the apparent truth that Shelleyan had been privy to the information but not him.

"You should really read it," Olivia said.

"You never finished it, liar," Shelleyan accused.

Olivia shrugged her off. "Of course I did."

"You just think he's cute," Shelleyan said. She turned to Charlie and he flinched. "He's in the movie for a second. He only has, like, one line."

Olivia giggled, embarrassed. "So what?" she asked. "He wrote the book it's based on, didn't he?"

"The book is nothing like the movie," Shelleyan snorted. "But I guess you wouldn't know that, huh?"

"So what?" Olivia said again. She had never found Shelleyan as intimidating as Charlie did.

He wondered how long it would be until she missed him. Really missed him, the way he knew he'd miss her once she was gone, a visa issue stripping her of her international student status after the spring semester. He dreaded the first time he would miss the candy aroma of her perfume, her smiling, freckled face drawing near, the harrowing moment when he would understand her loss in terms of his happy future thieved, stolen away back into the wilds of England.

Olivia had never mentioned Vernon Downs or *Minus Numbers* as far as he could recall, and he thought for a minute that they were putting him on. He awaited the punch line, the gentle ribbing that signified that he was still an intimate and not an ignorant outsider. He wasn't sure which he preferred: Olivia's having a simple infatuation with Downs or her actually admiring his writing, which, though he hadn't read anything by Downs, he was satisfied was facile and gimmicky. Hadn't he seen Downs in *GQ*? Serious writers didn't appear in the pages of *GQ*.

He was overcome with sadness at Olivia's leaving. Charlie knew intimately what it was to have something ripped out of your life, enervating your will, and senselessly: his parents, sure; but also the Kepharts, his maternal grandparents, in Denver, who helped him secure his Batman costume so he could burst into his third-grade homeroom, his new best friend, Jesse Mason, trailing in the Robin outfit, Mrs. Holstein looking on calmly as they scrambled after George McLean, the only Asian at Elrod Elementary, whom Charlie had talked into dressing as the Joker. The Kepharts had helped him crumple tiny pieces of aluminum foil, filling the bag of fake diamonds George clutched in his hand. Charlie's classmates squealed as the pursuit led them across the room, the chase continuing into the adjoining homeroom, as per his design. He explained to the principal that the drama would be more believable if the entire school was captivated by the play, a syllogism the principal accepted, much to Charlie's amazement. What Charlie didn't confess to the principal was that the production was simply a stunt to impress Suzy Young, whom he'd been caught kissing after the bell.

And the McCallahans, his aunt and uncle in Santa Fe, where he'd gone to live after the Kepharts admitted they were too old to raise a child. The McCallahans couldn't look at him with the same eyes they laid on their son, Ian, with whom Charlie had built a fort in the backyard out of empty boxes from Mr. McCallahan's job at Southwest Peterbilt. Only afterwards did he realize that Ian was technically his cousin, a fact that never arose while he was staying with the McCallahans.

And the Alexander-Degners of Rapid City, a cousin of his father's who was married to his high school sweetheart. Their childless neighbors had a dog that often found its way into the Alexander-Degners' yard. Charlie would play with the dog, chasing it up the grassy berm in their backyard that led to the freeway. The new neighbors were rarely seen, so that when a short, bearded man knocked on the Alexander-Degners' door to discuss erecting a fence between their yards to keep the dog from roaming free, Mr. Alexander assumed the man was the husband of the woman next door. Charlie learned only by eavesdropping that the man was a boyfriend, and that the couple had rented the house to get away from the woman's husband, a fact that the neighborhood discovered the morning after the boyfriend loaded his shotgun into his station wagon and drove to the local bar to call the husband outside and fire a slug into his chest, ending the alleged harassment the boyfriend and the woman next door had suffered at the husband's hands. The murder shocked their street, more so as no one knew the boyfriend or the woman, who had endeavored to live anonymously among their neighbors. Charlie retraced the neighbor's short drive to the bar in his mind, hearing him call the husband out onto the street, away from the innocent patrons, raising the shotgun to chest level. He imagined the husband, drunk, not begging for his life but daring the boyfriend to pull the trigger. Charlie heard the pop, smelled the smoke, saw the bewildered look on the husband's face. What were his taunts? How had he harassed them? Charlie tried to imagine the satisfaction the boyfriend must've felt when the threats evaporated. He wondered what it felt like to erase the past just like that.

He missed the Wallaces of San Diego too, another aunt and uncle, with whom he'd lived on base. Mr. Wallace treated him to trips to the flight simulator on Saturdays, until the Wallaces were dispatched to an air force base in Florida, a place Charlie, for some reason, couldn't go.

And of course he'd miss the Chandlers, his Arizona family, who'd enrolled him with every good intention at Randolph College Preparatory, an all-boys Jesuit high school of which Mr. Chandler was an alum. The Chandlers lived next door to his first cousin, twice removed, who agreed to take him in when the Wallaces left for Florida. The first cousin was a salesman for something called Simco and went missing for long stretches of time, leaving Charlie in the care of a succession of older women the first cousin called "friends." Charlie noticed the surfeit of kids living in the brown and white ranch next door and quickly found himself welcomed by the Chandlers, who were foster parents to six kids, including Talie, whom Charlie followed around like a puppy dog. With the first cousin's permission, the Chandlers helped Charlie file the paperwork to emancipate at seventeen, the family court judge scowling at him as if he were making the mistake of a lifetime, the glare lasting an uncomfortably long time, ruining the pizza party at Pistol Pete's that the Chandlers had thrown to help him celebrate his entree into adulthood.

Charlie had admitted his fractured past to Olivia and was relieved when she didn't consider him the alien in landscape he mostly felt in his day-to-day life. He anticipated the moment in any social scenario— especially potentially romantic ones—when his past would arise, which always required endless qualifications. He'd omitted the gaping hole in his life that was Jenny, the Mormon girl he'd met in high school. Jenny's sudden marriage just after she graduated was a wound that wouldn't heal, and Charlie was too embarrassed to admit to Olivia the hold his memories of Jenny held over him. Or his secret hope that Olivia would be the one that would make him forget about Jenny forever.

"Did you see he's coming to Phoenix?" Shelleyan asked. She pulled her reddish brown hair back and adjusted her scrunchie, revealing the dabs of sparkle she'd applied high on her cheeks. She didn't know it, but the joke among those students who knew her was whether or not they could get sparkled by Shelleyan. A few had, and still others dreamed of it.

Olivia's eyes grew wide. "You're lying."

"It was in the paper, dummy. He's got a new book coming out," Shelleyan said, gathering up her napkin and utensils. "No picture, though. He hates having his picture taken. Don't you read the paper?" Charlie hated the way all of Shelleyan's questions intimated that everyone else was in the know, and he suspected her questions were really aimed at him specifically, to dunce him in front of Olivia. "I gotta jet," she said, keeping one eye on Miles Buchanan, a hotel restaurant management major—and current focus of Shelleyan's affections—as he sauntered past the table and gave her a not-too-subtle wink, then drifted toward the door. Charlie guessed they were headed out to the parking lot, to make out in the backseat of Miles's silver Ford Bronco; Miles had told Shelleyan he'd tinted the windows with just those aspirations.

Lunch ended with Olivia promising to meet Charlie after classes, as usual, but he couldn't concentrate in his British literature class, distracted by the revelation about Vernon Downs. His need to be the center of Olivia's life flushed him with jealousy as he stared at the copy of *Pride and Prejudice* open on his desk, Professor Rudrud's words droning on. He hadn't been able to read the novel beyond the first few chapters, as the phrase "It is better to know as little as possible of the defects of the person with whom you are to pass your life" upset him so much that he couldn't continue, and he knew he would recall Austen's words verbatim every time he heard the book's title.

The plan to write Vernon Downs and arrange a private meeting while he was in Phoenix, lunch maybe, formed before the end of class. Charlie felt sure that Downs would agree to lunch, maybe dinner, with a couple of fans. He dogged it to the library, rounding the deserted stacks of the fiction section. He browsed the multicolored spines—Danticat, Dickens, Didion—halting when he saw the prize in the hunt, and reached for those by Vernon Downs. He arranged the books in a neat row in one of the study carrels, studying the covers, taking them in all at once, then focusing on the name Vernon David Downs as if trying to decode its mystery. He flipped the books over to reveal the author photo on each and was taken aback at how young the Vernon Downs who wrote *Minus Numbers* was. *He looks like a kid*, Charlie thought as he studied the cool pout, the tousled hair, the black and white suit. He marked his own passing resemblance to Vernon Downs and wondered if Olivia had a type. The author photo on the back cover of *Scavengers*, Downs's second book, was hardly recognizable—the hair a little less abundant, the lines under the eyes, a cardiganed Downs hunched over on the steps of a nondescript brownstone. The studio shot on the back of *The Vegetable King* featured Downs in profile, his chin tipped up like an actor on a movie poster. "The powerful new novel by the controversial author of *Minus Numbers* and *Scavengers*" ran above the photo in bold lettering. He wondered if Downs's reticence to be otherwise photographed was simple vanity, and was surprised at how much pleasure the thought afforded. Was he jealous of Vernon Downs? The real question superseded this: What did Olivia see in Vernon Downs? He would've given anything to know how Olivia had first discovered Vernon Downs. What had drawn her in? The primary-color book jackets, the author photo, what? The novels were seemingly about the rich and affected, a class of people he'd never known Olivia to be particularly enticed by. Olivia's stories in workshop were mostly realist and were gently criticized for occasionally lapsing into sentimentality. Charlie read into Olivia's work and gleaned from her fiction that she was someone who prized kindness and life's small coincidences over the themes of apathy and perversion that Downs seemed obsessed with.

He toted the books to the bank of gray metal microfiche projectors and ordered a spate of reels from the portly, skeptical student working the front desk, a worn copy of *Zen and the Art of Motorcycle Maintenance* splayed on the counter. Charlie wheeled through article after article about Vernon Downs, gathering and absorbing the biographical ephemera.

He began to unravel the mystery, the slow calculus computing. Vernon Downs wasn't a writer in the sense that other writers referenced in workshop were writers. Vernon Downs was as famous as the company he kept at nightclubs in New York, and restaurants in L.A. named Spago and Pastis and Bossa Nova. That he was a writer was incidental to his incredible celebrity.

Charlie couldn't calculate what excited him more: the prospect of arranging the lunch for Olivia, or announcing it in front of Shelleyan. In retrospect, he wished he hadn't been so confident in Vernon Downs's response, a confidence that tricked him into writing a short, breezy letter wherein he briefly described Olivia's admiration and their willingness to come to his hotel if that was more convenient. He cringed when he remembered his casual salutation—"Hey, Vernon"—that opened the letter, as if they were old friends. And he regretted not lying about his own admiration for Vernon Downs's books—he'd planned to catch the movie version of *Minus Numbers* so he could converse intelligently about the novel. Each minute after Charlie dropped the letter addressed to Vernon Downs in care of his publisher in the mailbox ticked by with a torpidity that bordered on cruelty.

He might've maintained his silence about the surprise, but circumstances conspired against him. First, the announced date for Downs's reading at Arizona State University was Valentine's Day, which lent his plan urgency. Then he opened the Sunday Arts section of the *Arizona Republic* to find the same studio shot of Vernon Downs from the back of *The Vegetable King*. The recognition felt personal, like seeing a picture of someone he knew. Just as startling as the photograph was the attendant article about the furor caused by the publication of *The Vegetable King*.

The elements of said furor seemed outrageous: sections of the book being leaked to *Time* magazine by staffers at Downs's publisher who were horrified by the content; a boycott instituted by the National Organization for Women because of the graphic torture and murder committed by the main character, Nick Banks; the pulping of the book by its original publisher, who allegedly bent to the will of its parent company, Gulf and Western, the book subsequently being snapped up, along with a short story collection called *The Book of Hurts*, by another publisher, which resulted in Downs being paid twice for the same book, Downs retaining the original six-figure advance. Charlie gulped back the information as quickly as he could, reading and rereading the article, converting the details into talking points whose vitality dimmed as the days expired without word from Vernon Downs. He knew the article would come up, and he even guessed correctly that Shelleyan would be the one to reference it. He had to wait only as long as Monday's lunch.

"That picture was hot," Shelleyan said. "He could be a model if he wanted."

"I can't wait to meet him." Olivia sipped her 7UP. "I don't care how long the line is." Abundant enthusiasm was just one of Olivia's attributes that enchanted him.

"Are you going to ask him to sign your book 'love'?" Shelleyan joked.

Olivia smirked at Shelleyan. "Very funny."

The words tumbled out before he could stop them. He hadn't heard so much as a word from Vernon Downs, but he felt his position in Olivia's life continually slipping as the date of her return home approached, and drastic action was the only recourse available to him.

"I was going to wait to tell you," he said, his temples pulsing, "but we're going to have lunch with him when he's in town. It's all arranged. I wrote to him and told him what a huge fan you are, and he's staying at the Phoenician—you know, the hotel on Camelback Mountain, really fancy, Madonna stays there when she's in town, so it must be . . ."—his breathing was so shallow he thought he might pass out, but he pressed on—"you know, pretty cool."

The look of astonishment on Olivia's face was worth every ounce of the lie, which didn't feel so much like a fabrication when Olivia jumped up and wrapped her arms around him, kissing him lightly on the cheek, a promise, he hoped, of more gratitude later. Charlie glanced at Shelleyan, whose quiet smile he purposely interpreted as jealousy and not the pure, undistilled doubt that she made no effort to conceal.

"You can get him to sign your book at lunch and avoid the lines," Shelleyan said drily.

As the weeks counted down to Vernon Downs's Phoenix appearance, Charlie nervously checked the mail with a frequency bordering on schizophrenic. He falsely accused his roommate, a stoner from Illinois who had dropped out of GCC the previous semester, of losing mail, making him promise not to visit the mailbox at all, for any reason. Worse, Shelleyan began alluding to the impending lunch with Vernon Downs with open hostility.

"What are you going to wear?" she asked Olivia at lunch one day in the cafeteria.

Another time: "Do you think he's a vegetarian? What if he orders, like, a salad?"

A week before the alleged lunch: "Ask him who designed the cover for the book. Tell him from me that it's pretty gross."

Charlie decided to take action. He called information for the phone number for Downs's publisher. He carried the number in his pocket for a day or two, allowing the mail one last chance to deliver salvation. Finally he called. The line rang just once before a sweet-sounding operator answered. Charlie mistook the person as an ally and confided his eagerness to treat his girlfriend to lunch with Vernon Downs (her favorite writer!) when he visited Phoenix next week. He may even have offered to pay for the lunch, in case the financial end of the thing was what was holding up a decision.

"Hello?" Charlie said after a short silence.

"You need to contact the author's agent," the operator said, all the succor drained from her voice. He timidly asked for that number, and after a lull where the real possibility that the operator had hung up loomed, she gave him the number for Downs's agent, Daar Baumann, and hung up. He held the phone long after the operator had clicked off, the name Daar Baumann resonating; it was listed in the acknowledgments of most of the important books published over the last decade or so.

"Can I say what this is regarding?" a mellifluous voice asked after he dialed the number he'd been given.

"Vernon Downs," he answered, trying to imitate a reporter, or some other persona that Downs's agent was comfortable dealing with. He yearned to better understand the foreign land he was touristing.

"One moment." The voice was suddenly replete with a dull apprehension.

Charlie self-consciously crossed his fingers during the silence, uncrossing them when the voice returned, flatter than before.

"She's in a meeting, can I take a message?"

He left a message, knowing it wouldn't be returned.

"Do you really think it would be okay to bring my book and get it signed?" Olivia asked as the phantom lunch date neared. "Or should I wait until the reading?" He nodded, searching for an equitable moment for confession. "Is it rude to bring more than one copy, do you think?" Her childlike worship might've infused a lesser man with jealousy, but Charlie only felt helplessness and defeat.

"I think it would be okay," he said.

He skipped classes the day before Vernon Downs's reading, trolling hotel switchboards, hoping to reach out to Downs personally. An hour or so spent calling the Phoenician and other luxury hotels in the metro Phoenix area, asking to leave a message for Vernon Downs, proved a fantastic waste of time, as none had a reservation under that name. He devised and then scuttled an elaborate plan whereby he'd take Olivia to an expensive restaurant and then claim Vernon had stood them up.

He would have to confess, simple as that. There was every chance that Olivia might be so angry with him that she would refuse his company thereafter. A night of fitful sleep left him agitated and hostile. He transferred his irritation at not being able to track down Vernon Downs to Shelleyan, brushing by her when she said, "Bummer, eh?"

"Fuck off," he grunted, prizing the shock on her face.

She called out after him, but a gaggle of administrators passed, drowning her out. He loitered in the parking lot to dodge the usual congregation in the cement amphitheater that functioned as the campus nerve center where he and Olivia and Shelleyan and others would meet before and after classes. He could successfully dodge Olivia until lunch, but lunch would bring its own set of problems, namely Shelleyan, and so he was skipping ahead after sociology when he spotted Olivia.

"Hey," she said. Her smile undid him and he feared abrupt tears, not only hers, but his. She opened her backpack and he spied her copies of *Minus Numbers* and *The Vegetable King*. She threw herself at him, her face buried in his chest. "It's so disappointing," she said, his secondhand Polo shirt muffling her cries.

The full import of what he'd done registered only then. "I know," he said. "I'm sorry." He'd hoped the simple confession would suffice, but he intuited that his future would be brimming with more contrition.

Olivia wiped a tear from her eye. "Stupid, right? I mean, think of Vernon. He's got it worse, right?"

The campus began to thin as he and Olivia moved dangerously toward tardiness. He tried not to betray that he didn't know how Vernon Downs had it worse. She passed him the carefully folded article from the *Phoenix Gazette* titled "Vernon Downs Cancels Tour." Charlie read with wonder as the article recounted what he already knew—the grim circumstances surrounding the publication of *The Vegetable King*—and what he didn't: the death threats, the organized protests, the stalker that showed up in city after city until rented bodyguards became a daily reality for the author.

He held the article gently, as if it were an archive document, or a religious parchment that held the divination pilgrims had been seeking their whole life. He handed it back to Olivia and grabbed her up in his arms, both to comfort her and to cloak his elation at having been so gloriously bailed out.

They consoled each other with repeated viewings of *Minus Numbers* at his apartment, exploiting Charlie's roommate's absence owing to a funeral in Michigan. They collaborated on a rebuttal to a scathing review in *Entertainment Weekly* of Downs's story collection, *The Book of Hurts*, published quickly to capitalize on the notoriety of *The Vegetable King*, and were elated when the magazine printed it in a subsequent issue:

> Once again a reviewer has overlooked the technical and literary genius of one of the brightest authors of our time, Vernon David Downs, whose work *does* represent the state of hip fiction today. We'll wager everyone who works at *EW* thinks Douglas Coupland is hip.
>
> —*Charlie Martens & Olivia Simmons, Phoenix*

The dig at Coupland, a popular writer, was especially satisfying to Charlie. His early investigation of Downs and his work had prompted him to class Downs and Coupland as the same kind of writer, but Olivia had begun preaching the virtues of Downs's work, the clinical satire, the wicked humor, the moral empathy at the heart of his seemingly immoral characters, and Charlie had been persuaded of Downs's talents.

A profile of Downs in *Vanity Fair* filled in the blanks about his canceled tour and gave an update about his whereabouts: He was ensconced in an unnamed town in Virginia with a friend, attempting to begin a new novel. The article described Downs as "bulky," a detail in direct opposition to his author photo, but didn't include any photographs, instead employing a full-page caricature emphasizing Downs's cherubic features. The odd detail of Downs picking up a bath towel and sniffing it to see if it was clean stayed with Charlie longer than it should've.

"Let's write him a letter," Olivia said. "A real fan letter. I've never written a true fan letter."

Charlie convinced her the better idea was to write a letter to the editor of *Vanity Fair*. "He might see it," Charlie reasoned.

Olivia crafted a note she hoped Downs would read, rejoiced when it appeared:

> Finally a quasi-revealing profile (as much as we'll ever know, I'll bet) of one of the most talented writers of our time. As a creative-writing student at Glendale Community College, I can say that Mr. Downs is among the most revered authors of my generation, admired for the fluidity of his prose style and his eye for context and detail, which, on the surface, appear ordinary enough but are really, under Mr. Downs's microscope, threatening and truly unnerving. I quiver with anticipation for the arrival of his latest masterpiece.
>
> —*Olivia Simmons, London*

The sexual innuendo of the last sentence bothered Charlie like an itch he couldn't reach, but he was more troubled by Olivia's identifying herself as a Londoner, a reminder that she was but a provisional visitor who would return to her homeland in a matter of months. He suppressed those emotions and they spent the next few days driving around the metro Phoenix area, buying up copies of *Vanity Fair*.

....

The idling cab, pulled to the curb at Summit Terrace, was a cocoon: Once Charlie stepped from it, the final act of his plan to win back Olivia would begin. Camden had been a trial run—everyone in the summer writing program would forever associate him with Vernon Downs and vice versa. The stage was bigger now. How to replicate the effect, he wasn't exactly sure. Olivia's words—"We can't see each other anymore"—still rattled him, though increasingly he thought of them as a challenge. He'd said he'd come the first chance he could, which meant financially, which was easily solved by an afternoon spent filling out preapproved credit card applications offered along with free T-shirts at various tables around campus. As the cards began to appear in the mail, he planned his trip to London and was devastated and confused when his weekly phone call didn't find Olivia at home. When he finally reached her, he wouldn't hang up without an explanation, and Olivia gave him an unbelievable one she had clearly contrived under duress. Perhaps her parents had learned about how she'd switched enrollment from Arizona State to Glendale Community College and were punishing her.

A desperate scenario in which he'd locate Vernon Downs in New York emerged. What would happen after that was anyone's guess, but he let himself be guided by impulse. He charged a one-way trip to New York City and studiously pored over a map on the flight, wondering where along the colored grid he'd find Vernon Downs. He traced the route from LaGuardia into the city so he wouldn't be taken advantage of by the unscrupulous taxi drivers of popular imagination. He laughed now as he remembered the look of surprise on the cabbie's face when Charlie instructed him to take the Triborough Bridge. He hadn't known that the Triborough was a toll bridge and that the Midtown Tunnel was the faster, free alternative. Other surprises lay in store, like the hotel in Times Square that was really a hostel, necessitating a pair of flip-flops from the corner CVS in order to use the communal shower; and how everything in New York cost at least two dollars more than it did in Phoenix. But the biggest surprise was the absolute lack of any trace of Vernon Downs anywhere in Manhattan. All the articles he'd read had Downs starring in nightly debaucheries, but as Charlie haunted the entrances of bars like Nell's and Balthazar and clubs like Tunnel and Limelight, he understood that everyone who entered those venues did so seeking debauchery. He stood squinting up at the office of Downs's literary agent, Daar Baumann, but knew nothing but disappointment awaited inside. Recognizing dead ends was a useful skill he'd developed early on.

The stench of defeat dogged him until a new plan spontaneously emerged, based on a flyer for a summer writing conference at Camden College, Downs's alma mater, that was stuck on a bulletin board at the New School, where Charlie had taken refuge from an early blast of summer heat. Camden had figured prominently in a number of Downs's books, and the conference featuring lectures and writing workshops would at the very least bring Charlie closer to the world of Vernon Downs. It seemed like the logical next step in his quest to win back Olivia.

....

Charlie cursed himself for scrimping, the late arrival time the result of a cheaper red-eye ticket that imprisoned him at the Albany bus station until six a.m., the first available pickup time that could be arranged by the car service, the only means of travel available to the remote college campus. This rookie mistake was obvious in retrospect as he trudged in circles through the tiny terminal, willing the sun to appear. He contemplated a hotel room, but the balance on one of his MasterCards had crept perilously toward the limit, and he vowed to eschew unnecessary purchases. He'd wait it out. He clutched the postcard of the Empire State Building he'd purchased at the Port Authority, debating about sending it. Olivia would see the beseeching lines he'd scrawled and know his longing for reconciliation. He slid the postcard into a mail slot and immediately began to worry that Olivia's parents would find the missive in the mail and trash it instead of delivering it to its intended reader.

He curled up on an uncomfortable half bench, the strap of his duffel bag looped around his arm to prevent robbery; the suede pouch within, given to him by the Kepharts, secreted keepsakes from his travels and was the sole possession he valued. He longed for the comfort of his bed back in Phoenix, though he knew his ex-roommate had found someone to rent his room after Charlie announced his plans to go east. Sleep came fitfully and then was banished forever by the whir of an industrial vacuum cleaner as the terminal underwent an early-morning cleaning. Six o'clock was forever in arriving, and despite his excitement at escaping the bus terminal, he dozed off in the back of the hired Lincoln Town Car, waking to marvel at the Vermont countryside. The sun glinted off the green fields and he took in the rural landscape.

The car sailed through a red-planked covered bridge eroded by time, the verdant landscape filtering in through the latticework, the car's interior spotted with sunlight. The Town Car shot out the yawning mouth of the bridge, delivering them into the town of Camden, a picturesque New England hamlet populated with wide lawns running back toward quiet houses nestled far from the road. The driver nosed the car through the gates of Camden College, itself set deep in the woods. An admixture of anxiety and excitement coursed through Charlie as the car crept along College Drive, finally slowing to a stop at the Barn, the two-story structure that functioned as the administration building. The driver let him off, and he signed for the service and the tip, which was more than he'd anticipated. He watched the black car drive away until it turned the corner, a curtain of morning sunlight falling over the still campus. The buildings appeared deserted: the Commons ahead and Crossett Library to his left, the manicured Commons lawn a quiet runway extending toward the End of the World, the abrupt terminus from which endless miles of Vermont woods and sky were visible.

He wondered what Olivia would say.

He wished he could know.

The single thought that he was finally within the inviting bosom of Vernon David Downs's alma mater was surreal. His sole preoccupation on the bus ride from New York had been how to breach the campus successfully—he'd run several scenarios involving multiple deceptions to finesse any security—and once the awe at how easily he'd been able to infiltrate

Camden had subsided, he realized he knew very little about Downs's existence on campus. Which of the green and white clapboard dorms had he lived in? McCullough? Booth? He set his bag down on one of the picnic tables outside of the Commons, distressed by extreme weather and extreme temperaments, searching the campus for any sign of life. *Vernon Downs probably sat at this picnic table*, he thought. He tried the door to Stokes, surprised when the handle gave easily, and roamed through the vacant dorm, choosing an empty room down an empty hall farthest from the entrance as his own. *He probably stared out this window*, Charlie thought. The distant mountaintops retained their snowy caps, even in the summer. *He may even have lived in this very room*, he thought as he drifted off to sleep, exhaustion washing over him as he spread out fully clothed on the soft bed.

Faint laughter woke him some time later. He squinted at the bluing light as he tried to gauge where he was. The gauzy curtains blew in the evening breeze, the air suffused with a floral sweetness. Out his window, dark figures moved against the gray landscape, some struggling with overpacked bags, others darting furtively in and out of their dorm, unpacking idling cars double-parked on the single-lane road that wound past the student housing.

His fellow Camdenites had finally arrived.

Charlie hurriedly showered and dressed, then sauntered toward the Commons, which cast rectangles of light across the darkening lawn, the destination of the flow of people appearing in doorways or emerging in tributaries from points unseen. He kept his head low, hoping to blend with those who were actually enrolled in the summer program. Experience had taught him that he could persuade people he was invisible, which invariably emboldened him in any new social situation, so he was bewildered by how nervous he felt. He followed a woman in her eighties wrapped in an oversized yellow Windbreaker, as if expecting a storm, into a dimly lit room crowded with amiable and eager faces, all congregated at a long wooden bar stocked with self-serve beer and wine, which was being grabbed up by nervous hands. Charlie tried to mix into the crowd, cradling a sweaty bottle of Budweiser, listening in on conversations that cut violently from how hard it was to find time to write, to a short list of favorite books, to which of the teachers huddled near the dormant stone fireplace was the recent National Book Award winner.

Camden's recent history was very much on everyone's minds too. Charlie gathered the bits and pieces of conversation to sew the narrative together: Just a year before, the college had taken the extraordinary step of abolishing tenure, firing a third of the professors who taught at Camden, invoking the ire and censure of the academic community. The air was polluted with uncertainty about Camden's future, which provided the perfect cover for Charlie's impersonation of a Camden student. He quickly fell into the proscribed banter, asking people where they were from, if they wrote fiction or poetry or what. He readily provided answers when the same was asked of him, sometimes recycling answers he'd been given moments before during a similar inquiry. There was something intoxicating about rotating in a crowd of aspirants. Anything was possible. Even getting Olivia back.

That night, he dreamed what he would do.

Early the next morning, he strolled into the Barn and located the alumni office.

"I'm a student here and would like the address for an alum," he said to the straw-thin girl with wispy blond hair behind the counter. "Vernon Downs." A rising nervousness pulsed through him. He regretted betraying his earlier instinct to employ a believable ruse. He'd considered several on the walk to the alumni office: that he was with the local newspaper and wanted to interview Downs; that he worked in the library and needed to forward a package someone had sent Downs; or that someone at the campus bookstore wanted to ship a carton of *The Vegetable King* to Downs for autographing. But none of the deceptions appealed to him, and it was better to go in straight than to proffer a lie he wasn't completely invested in.

"I'm just watching the desk for my friend," the girl said. "I actually work in admissions."

"Oh," Charlie said. He leaned on the counter in what he hoped was an unassuming pose. "Which is better?"

The girl made a face. "Both are boring," she answered. "But it beats working in the cafeteria with the rest of the losers."

Charlie laughed. "I suppose it does." The girl glanced absently at the clock on the wall, the red second hand gliding slowly across its face. "I like the food here," he said. "I mean, I like that someone else takes care of it."

The girl smiled. "I'm a vegan, so I only really eat at the salad bar."

Charlie worried that his request would come under scrutiny if the girl's friend reappeared, and he debated leaving. But something in the way the girl behind the counter nervously began to scratch her elbow betrayed that she and her friend were likely up to something, or she was worried that she'd be found out for spelling her friend, who was off doing who knew what, and Charlie reversed course.

"I'm sort of in a hurry," he said, affecting impatience.

"God, where is she?" the girl asked. "She's been gone for, like, ten minutes."

"Is there someone else who can help me?" Charlie asked, searching the obviously empty office.

"I'll just do it," she said. The girl tapped something on the computer. She handed him a yellow Post-it note, a phone number scrawled in her slanted handwriting. "It says the request for an updated address is pending, sorry." Charlie thanked her and memorized the phone number in case something disastrous happened to the Post-it, which he folded into his wallet, with the intention of transferring it to the safety of the suede pouch. He absented the alumni office quickly, as if he might be called back to account, the creaky floorboards singing underfoot. An errant left brought him face-to-face with the director of the summer program, a large bearded Irishman with tortoiseshell glasses whom he recognized from the writing program flyer.

"Hello," the director boomed.

Charlie gave a short wave, an understatement he hoped the director would let stand.

"Good man," the director said, slapping him heartily on the back, which propelled him in an unplanned direction, around the nearest corner and away from the director, who bounded out the door and into the brightening sky. Charlie strolled down the hall strewn with cluttered corkboards and stacks of unstained wooden chairs, hunting for an exit that would circumvent the director and thus avert an embarrassing conversation he was sure neither of them wanted to have.

A murmuring wafted through the breezy hallway, and Charlie slowed at the open door bearing an engraved plastic plaque advertising the summer writing program office. He feigned interest in the flyers pushpinned to the bulletin board outside the door while straining to hear.

"We should make them pay when we accept them," a voice tinged with anger said. "That would keep them from dropping out without notice."

"They'd just want a refund," a smaller voice said. "There's no way to guarantee they'll show up."

"But canceling at the last minute," the first voice countered. "If he would've had to pay in full, that would've forced him to attend."

Charlie lifted an outdated flyer about summer studies abroad and focused on an announcement about a film series at the local cinema featuring movies inspired by books. Some days the fantasy that Olivia could see him was all he had to motivate him, and her phantom presence had become so ingrained that he often acted as if he were on a stage, with the audience just off in the wings.

"The workshops are all screwed up now," the first voice said, exasperation replacing anger.

"Can't we draft the closest wait lister?" the small voice said.

"Not at this late date," was the reply.

Charlie stared dumbly at the bulletin board. He had what he'd come for, and extending his stay on campus could only increase the chance of exposure. But there was an allure about all he didn't know about Vernon Downs and his time at Camden. He reasoned that an education in All Things Vernon could only aid in his overall goal to ingratiate himself with the author. Plus, it was more economically feasible to spend ten days in Vermont than ten days in New York City. He crept away from the open door, the floor creaking underfoot, threatening to expose him as he formulated what exactly he'd say. He didn't consider it lying, exactly, but an expedience that benefited all parties involved—a cousin to a white lie, or at best, an act of charity whose currency was simple, harmless untruths.

He circled the Barn, gathering courage before striding into the writing program office. The air-conditioning had been turned low and Charlie shivered as he approached the counter.

"Can I help you?" The small voice he'd heard earlier belonged to a round, dour woman behind a wooden desk weighted down with stacks of shuffled papers and a computer monitor three technologies old.

"I need to pay my tuition," he said confidently, smiling sheepishly, as if the joke was on him in some way.

"What's the name?" the woman asked as she pulled a pair of reading glasses from her worn sweater.

He gave her his name and she typed it slowly into the computer. A dark figure moved behind a pane of frosted glass in the door guarding an inner office. The dour woman frowned. "I don't have you in my computer," she said.

Charlie smiled casually, knowing this was the critical performance. "Maybe I'm still on the wait list," he suggested. "I was wait-listed at first." He rubbed his hands together and then dropped them to his sides, shrugging in a mimic of a small child waiting instruction from a parent.

The woman clacked the keys of her computer again, a look of consternation on her face. "Hmm," she said, and Charlie could see the conceit he'd planted in her mind take bloom. "Wait one moment, please." She swept out of the room, easing behind the door to the inner office, which was consumed with urgent whispering. The door opened and closed again, and the woman rounded her desk, a curiously thin file folder in her hand. "Found it," she said, sighing dramatically. "Computers can't beat a good old-fashioned filing system."

Charlie chortled dutifully. "They never will," he agreed, nodding at the prop file. He was amazed but not surprised that the trick had worked.

"How would you like to pay?" the woman asked.

Charlie placed his MasterCard on the counter, and the woman fished a carbon from the top drawer. He smiled as she copied down his credit card number, confident that the summer writing conference would be over before the transaction was processed, at which point he would call MasterCard and refute the charges, feigning ignorance about what or where Camden was.

Charlie moved into the cramped room assigned him in Booth, no longer having to squat in Stokes on the fringe of the summer program, though his official admittance left him feeling exposed. He nodded politely to the girl who lived at the end of the hall, alarmed that she'd try to trap him in a conversation about books or writing. A low-level fear accompanied him as he rotated on the outside of groups of students that formed and broke apart with the speed of supernovas. His artistic resume—two semesters of creative writing at Glendale Community College—represented the least distinguished credentials among those in attendance, who all seemed either to be enrolled at Iowa or Columbia or Williams, or to have decades of life experience, which lent an air of authority to their theories about writing and what constituted art.

Workshop was another matter entirely. He spent evenings in his room conscientiously reading the stories passed out that afternoon. The quality of the stories was markedly better than those he'd seen at GCC—several read as smoothly as published stories—and he couldn't find anything substantive to say, so that by the third meeting, he was the lone participant who hadn't spoken, forcing Jane Martin, the workshop leader and author of a famous book set in an eponymous small town, to call on him. He fumbled through a string of exhortations about the quality of the writing and plotting, aping speech he'd heard in the hallways and dining room, finally making an original point about the likability of the narrator, a widowed herpetologist who falls in love with a woman half his age. The con held, though he wasn't sure that all his workshop mates were convinced he belonged there, a suspicion he feared would be confirmed as the deadline for him to hand in his story approached. His small cache of original work was archived on a blue diskette he kept in the suede pouch, and he reread everything he'd written on a computer in Crossett Library, but none of it exhibited the quality of the work they'd been considering at Camden. One of the first stories he'd written, "My Last Jenny," was too upsetting to finish reading. Another, about people all over the country mistakenly spotting Lee Harvey Oswald in the moments after the Kennedy assassination, rose in his estimation, but the story was too personal, written during a sensitive time—he hadn't even shared it with Olivia—and he wasn't eager to hear it dissected in workshop.

The situation plagued him all through the field trip arranged by Jane Martin for the purpose of an elaborate writing exercise designed around the tragic disappearance of Paula Jean Welden, the Camden sophomore who walked out into the campus woods in the mid-1940s and vanished.

Charlie tramped along the worn trail, the campus receding behind the group of students lacquered with astringent bug spray. They listened as Jane Martin described Paula Jean's disappearance, how she'd marched out the front gates in the December cold without a jacket or scarf, how a garage owner closing for the night was the last to see her alive, if you discounted the bus driver who claimed Paula Jean had grabbed the last bus to New York City, or the waitress at the Modern Café who swore she'd served Paula Jean a plate of scrambled eggs and sausage with a side of pancakes.

"The rumor that she was underdressed led searchers to believe that Paula Jean was rendezvousing with someone who had a car or a cabin," Jane Martin said. She gathered the group under a stand of birch trees, the sunlight spotting the faces of the would-be scribes, anxious to please. "So take out your notebooks," Jane Martin said, "and sketch out a few paragraphs about what you think happened to Paula Jean."

Notebooks and pens were wrestled free of bags and backpacks. Charlie took out a pocket-size Camden notebook he'd shoplifted in the campus bookstore. He held his pen to paper like a reporter but drew a blank. The other workshoppers scribbled furiously, constructing whole lies out of the scraps of a girl's unsolved disappearance. Charlie found it exhausting to speculate about Paula Jean, a little disconcerted that the others found it so easy. Weren't they worried that adopting a tendency to fabricate would leak over into their real lives? The girl standing opposite him swatted at a red spot on her tanned leg with her notebook.

Jane Martin called time and all but a few pens stopped scratching out make-believe. "Who wants to go first?" she asked.

Predictably, the eager, bird-faced brunette from Wisconsin, whose workshop story was roundly criticized for flowery language and corny sentiment, shot her hand in the air.

"Go ahead, Charisse," Jane Martin said without a hint of reluctance. Charlie wondered how a professional and published writer like Jane Martin could summon the patience for wannabes like Charisse and the others in the group. The only legitimate answer was the amount of the paycheck, he surmised.

Charisse proceeded with a spiel about Paula Jean and a mystery lover, taking the obvious cue and running. In Charisse's version, the mystery lover was a disfigured local boy whom Paula Jean had befriended. Longing to shrug off their shackles—in Charisse's take, Paula Jean was sick of being rich and bored—they plunged deep into the woods to live simply and shirk the value system imposed on them by a superficial society. "I didn't get to finish," Charisse lamented. "I think they had children, too, who they raised accordingly."

Charlie suffered through an outpouring of implausible plotlines involving UFOs, Bigfoot, kidnappers, and sinkholes. Jane Martin tried to convey that the *how* was less interesting than the *why*, compelled to hold up Charisse's ridiculous response as an example of interior versus exterior. He understood perfectly what she was trying to impart. He thought about Paula Jean leaving all that she was behind, trusting in the unknown. How fearful she must've been that she'd be caught, dragged back to the present she was trying to outrun, consigned to the life she wanted to give back.

Paula Jean's struggle was mighty compared with his own life, Charlie realized. How easily had he slipped from place to place, a new set of friends, a new school, everything new, new, new? Pride surged within him as he realized how much Paula Jean would've envied his life. The fresh slant on his own history enthralled him until the gross similarities between Paula Jean's disappearance into the Vermont woods and his exodus from Denver, and Santa Fe, and Rapid City, and San Diego, struck him. The bothersome thought that he could simply walk away from Phoenix, and from Olivia and the memories they shared, couldn't be dislodged from his mind, no matter how distasteful the idea. He refused to surrender to the hypothesis, afraid of the power of admission. It was like using a relative's death as a fake excuse for missing school—once proffered, the evitable would follow. To forget Olivia would be to forsake the one person who could provide his one real chance to quit the dizzying carousel of towns and fleeting friendships that had accrued over the years. He lamented surrendering his apartment, his only real tether to Phoenix, even though he'd had to financially. He'd never doubled back before and had discounted its comfort as a fallback. An afternoon wind rustled the leaves, and he clung to his memories of Olivia, battered by the awareness foisted upon him by the stupid writing exercise. An outer dark loomed beyond the group of workshoppers, the bleak future that awaited Charlie if he succumbed to cataloging Olivia as just another person in another town that he'd known.

He heard his name called, Jane Martin bringing him back from the precipice. The group eyed him, waiting, but he shrugged. "I couldn't think of anything," he said, closing his notebook.

....

Charlie strode across the short, thick grass of the Commons lawn, glancing up in time to avert being hit by a stray shuttlecock from a scratch badminton game being played by other Camdenites, all of whom were swatting at the birdie with their free hand, the other hand minding their full plastic cup of wine or beer. The campus was in its postdinner lull, the sun still high in the sky, the faculty readings still hours away. An esprit de corps had enveloped the campus, and those with cars motored into Camden to haunt the shops for trinkets for their children or significant others, or to stock up on the basic necessities at the newly constructed Wal-Mart. Charlie had skipped dinner to stroll around the fetid pond and through the tall, ragged grass of Jennings Meadow, which led to Jennings Hall, the granite mansion that housed the music facilities. The summer writing program was mostly contained at the other end of campus, and the foot traffic on the trail to Jennings thinned noticeably as he broached the imposing house. He'd overheard vague tales about how Jennings was haunted, how music students practicing in the converted studios would hear strange, unmusical noises that would chase them back to their dorms and trouble their dreams, but he didn't believe in the supernatural and dismissed the rumors as campus mythology.

A rush of wind blew across the naked meadow and he turned his back to it, his T-shirt and shorts billowing in the gale. The warm air cooled as it subsided, swaying the maple saplings that ringed the mansion. He listened for music—a prim group who ate at a table in the windowless corner of the dining hall were rumored to be music students stranded at Camden

for the summer—but Jennings was quiet. The front door caught when
he tried it. He read about the Jennings family on the historical marker
bolted to the stone facade, about how Mr. Jennings had been a powerful lawyer in New York City who died in his midsixties, widowing his
wife, who ultimately donated the house for the creation of Camden College, a Depression-era college for women. The engraved words EST. 1880
appeared in smaller type at the bottom of the plaque, and Charlie ran his
hand over them, his fingers lingering over the numbers, the one and the
eights and the zero. *More than a hundred years old*, he mused. *Older than
the state of Arizona.* He thought of the hastily abandoned Mrs. Jennings
and shuddered. Without warning, the parade of friends he'd left behind
filed through his mind. He'd made widows of them all as he bounced here
and there. He was curious to know if he'd left a trail of heartbreak. He'd
never before considered that his previous experiences and relationships
were anything more than finite—their separateness had given him pleasure, the compilation of memories a zoetrope always spinning in his mind.
That he'd been a bit player in an array of people's lives, against a myriad
of backgrounds, seemed impossible. Yet he acknowledged the probability
that he hadn't widowed anyone, but simply passed through their lives with
an inconsequential nod and a polite smile.

....

   The end of Charlie's time at Camden was marked with turmoil. As he
stood in Tishman, the subterranean lecture hall, barely looking up from
the lectern, he was unable to measure the audience's enthusiasm for his
selection for the recreational after-dinner readings. Most read selections
from authors that had made them want to become writers, and Charlie
was enamored of the idea of lineage. He became obsessed with publicly
sharing what had led him to Camden, associating himself with Downs in
the minds of others.
   Vernon Downs was by far one of the most successful writers in Camden's

history, but his name was whispered in the halls with a mix of shame and admiration. By comparison, students talked loudly about Bernard Malamud, who had taught at Camden for decades; or Robert Frost, who had lived in a house on campus and was buried nearby; or Jamaica Kincaid, who lived in a beautiful wood house behind the campus. But no one ever spoke openly about Downs. Charlie silently dedicated the reading to Olivia, then began, immediately recognizing that he'd started reading the wrong page. He'd intended to read a comic scene involving business cards but had inexplicably opened the book to a scene that included one of the most violent passages in *The Vegetable King*. As he neared the conclusion of the reading, he gazed out awkwardly and smiled at the applause. He was aware that some had walked in late—the lecture hall doors had swung open and shut loudly during the reading.

Mike Conway, who occupied the suite opposite his and with whom he'd exchanged pleasantries, approached. "Did you hear those people walking out?" he asked.

"What do you mean?" Charlie asked.

"When you started reading the part about the rat, a bunch of women got up and walked out."

Mike approached him again at breakfast the next morning. "There's something on the bulletin board in Commons you might want to read," he said solemnly. Previously, the bulletin board had served as a collage of cartoons cut from the pages of the *New Yorker* or anonymous diatribes about laundry room etiquette, so the sober note Mike struck was troubling.

Charlie followed him to Commons, and they waited for the group of students clustered around the bulletin board to disperse before stepping up. Charlie scanned the letter tacked in the center of the board.

I am deeply offended by Charlie Martens's public reading of Vernon Downs's work. Downs has the right to write what he chooses, Martens has the right (in the privacy of his own mind) to read what he chooses. I also have the right <u>not</u> to fill my mind with graphic depictions of sexualized violence against women. To be subjected to such images out of the blue (images I may never be able to erase from my thoughts) is a violation.

As writers, we are all concerned with freedom of speech, but Martens crossed the line—his action was disrespectful and unacceptable. I, for one, take issue with what he did—I protest.

The note had been annotated by others, the addendums written in different-colored inks:

I agree (and I had previously read the passage out of <u>choice</u>).

It would have been nice to have had the option to leave the room (or go read the passage myself if I wanted) before this gratuitous reading. It was nothing less than mental rape.

I agree. What was the point?

Mike told Charlie not to worry about it. Mike's dismissive attitude comforted him, though for the rest of the day Charlie felt like others were staring at him. He assuaged his discomfort by telling himself the letter was a stunt that would die by lunch, an idea he believed until a follow-up letter was posted:

1. Charlie Martens could have offered a handout of the VDD passage, then any consequent debate would have been, as it should have been, about <u>it</u>, not about his method of presentation.

2. This debate isn't about censorship, but about courtesy, specifically about ways of demonstrating respect for others' sensibilities.

3. Providing those of "tender sensibilities" an opportunity to leave would not have been a good solution. The image of women rising + leaving raises attendant images of women withdrawing from men after dinner—to the (with)drawing room. A solution that literally separated us would be no solution at all. Isn't common ground a precondition of community?

Followed by another:

The material of Vernon David Downs is strong, unpleasant, and to my mind, not very important, which is why I chose not to attend. But should what is presented here be shaped to the most vulnerable among us? With all respect for the sensitivities of those who find the material offensive, as a woman I find it ironic that we seem on the verge of returning to the time when someone else decided, "The material is a bit rough. Perhaps the ladies would like to step outside," or even worse, to a time when in the back rooms others would say, "This material is something that might be important to hear, but in deference to the ladies, we can't even consider it."

I didn't come here to be protected, thank you.

Charlie's reading and the bulletin board postings were the rage in the dorms and on campus. His paranoia about being gawked at was validated as his peers averted their eyes whenever he attempted to make eye contact in lecture. He began skipping lectures in favor of camping out in his room. The cafeteria became an arena of liability too when an older woman he'd never seen before accosted him, leaning in so that her face nearly grazed his. "I think you're disgusting," she said. She waited for a reaction of some kind, but he just shrugged, knowing he could not convince her otherwise.

Charlie considered vanishing, but he had begun scratching out notes for a story based on his relationship with Olivia and wondered if work-shopping the story might bring some clarity about his situation. So for the rest of the conference, Charlie attached himself to various groups revolving through campus, trickling into pools of conversation, mostly unnoticed, though he affected an agreeable tone when included in whatever was being discussed. It seemed that while everyone had heard about the public outcry over his reading of Downs's work, very few people actually knew Charlie by sight. Right when the controversy threatened to wane, the soap-operatic narrative folding in on itself—where people stood on the

issue boiled down to whether or not they were fans of Downs's work—
Mike knocked on his door.

"There's something you should see," he said.

Charlie read over the shoulders of the group gathered around the
bulletin board:

Dear Charlie,

It may please you to know that Vernon David Downs went down fighting.
As I fed the first page of The Vegetable King into the fire, a cluster of flames
leaped out from beneath the paper and scalded my thumb. He went down
like the condemned man before the firing squad, spitting in the soldiers'
faces. What else can they do to him? Vernon did not beg or bribe or whim-
per. He took his punishment like a man.

But we burned him like women. Gently. Not like Nazis burned books,
with the false and grandiose notion that we can actually eradicate the text,
the idea, the memory. No, we burned him the way a woman burns the letters
of an ex-lover. The way a woman burns the letters of an ex-lover when she
has lost him to violence—his. She burns them gently, grieving for her lost
innocence. She knows now that loving can be dangerous. Just as listening
can be dangerous. Trusting the words of your soft mouth not to harden like
a hand that once caressed hardens into a fist.

We cannot unbruise our ears from this or any other unwanted intrusion.
Vernon David Downs has carved his initials into us like the trunks of trees.
But we burned the pages and called the names of women. Strangers, women
we know, women we love, women in our families, who have been raped or
beaten or brutalized. Real women, not the inexhaustible legions of women
in fiction who offer themselves up willingly. Real women.

I am lucky. I have a voice that tells me everything important. Shortly after your
reading began, it told me to leave. Now, I was comfortable, and it was humid out.
But one of my favorite gospel songs says, "I'm gonna do what the Spirit say do."
Spirit said leave, so I did. I didn't hear the passages you read, but I saw them in

the distressed faces of the women who are my friends and colleagues.

Is that why the flames chose my hand as we sacrificed Vernon into the fire? Was it because I had been unscathed by the words? Maybe it was a reminder that although we are right, the element of fire does not prefer Vernon's flesh over mine. Perhaps it was to remind me that burning Vernon wasn't without danger.

After we finished, one of my friends gave me a clear plastic cup of ice water. As I rewound the tape in my cassette player, I stuck my thumb into the cup to soothe the burn. Then we played Queen Latifah's "U.N.I.T.Y." and danced.

We won this little battle, but not because we burned The Vegetable King. We won because despite the infinite number of tortures real women experience every day, we are also real women, and we were with each other, and we were making ritual, and we were dancing.

It didn't take long for news of the ritualistic burning to sweep across campus. Conversations were held in muted tones. There were those among the population who were appalled by the act and expressed their opinion vocally; others were equally appalled by Charlie's presence, and their silent glaring communicated their disgust. The entire student body was enveloped in a foul stink. The reactions were too extreme for Charlie to register them as anything other than self-aggrandizing, though he secretly relished the episode as the twinning of his narrative with Vernon's.

....

Charlie thought to review his questions in the cab, but he'd memorized them—even their order—and didn't want to sully the reporter's notebook he'd charged at the stationery store in Union Square as a backup to the mini recorder he intended to return with the receipt to the electronics store near Grand Central Station. As the hands on his watch moved

toward ten, he was seized with worry: Were his loafers too weathered?
Was his haircut cool enough? Did he look like a poor student on financial
aid, or could he somehow pass as the sort of hipster Downs wrote about
and probably socialized exclusively with? *Don't come off as too eager*, he ad-
monished himself, knowing a misstep could halt the forward progress
he'd made since leaving Phoenix. He ducked under the green and white
awning of Summit Terrace, the doorman nodding as he pushed through
the etched glass door.

"Yes?" the doorman asked, balancing a copy of the *Village Voice* on his lap.

"I'm here to see Vernon Downs," Charlie said carefully.

"Name?" the doorman asked.

"Vernon Downs," Charlie repeated.

"No," the doorman said sourly. "*Your* name."

He gave his name and the doorman announced his arrival in the receiver of the white phone on the desk. "Okay," the doorman said into the
mouthpiece. "Okay." He hung up. "He's not ready for you yet. Be five
minutes."

Charlie paced the octagonal brick and glass lobby, the strong urge to
urinate visiting him. "Do you have a bathroom?" he asked.

"Basement," the doorman said. "Door by the elevator."

He followed the passageway to the maintenance room but was so
paranoid that Vernon would descend and find the lobby empty that the
emergency abandoned him and he retreated. "You can go up," the doorman said without looking at him.

The ride to the fourth floor was short, and Charlie nearly fainted as
he raised a tremulous fist to knock on Vernon's door. The journey from
Phoenix to New York to Camden to Summit Terrace had been longer than he had expected, riddled with setbacks he could never have
anticipated on the bus from Vermont. His previous foray into Manhattan
had in no way prepared him for life on the East Coast. He didn't possess
the skills to procure the kind of job necessitated by astronomical rent and

utility payments, a riddle that vexed him as he ambled the city streets, down skyscraper-lined Fifth Avenue, to the South Street Seaport, over to Wall Street, and back up the West Side, cutting over to Central Park and looping through the Great Lawn. He avoided the subway, certain that it was a death sentence based on the wild rumors he'd heard growing up in the West about murder after murder being committed on the tracks, until he counted up the colossal sums he was spending on cab fare and forced himself to take public transportation. The roar of the hot subway was more exhilarating than expected, and once he effected his first successful transfer at Times Square, he felt he was mastering the art of life in New York.

His living situation had finally stabilized too. A brief stay at the Holiday Inn in Midtown maxed out one of his MasterCards and he checked out, leaving the cut-up plastic remains in the wastebasket. Charlie traipsed around Manhattan, realizing quickly that if he wanted a place to live, he'd be relegated to one of the less fashionable boroughs, either Queens or the Bronx, maybe Staten Island. He rode the N train to Astoria, a heavily Greek neighborhood in Queens, and spent an afternoon climbing the stairs in prewar apartment buildings to look at all there was for rent. Astoria's proximity to Manhattan had corrupted rent prices, so that renters were being shuttled deeper into Long Island City, or to New Jersey. Dismayed, Charlie boarded the N train back into the city, hatching a fallback plan wherein he'd ride the subway all night with the other homeless if it should come to that.

A stopgap solution revealed itself in the form of the night front desk position at the Yale Club, but he was fired after two days when the day manager caught him sleeping in one of the well-appointed guest rooms, a sleep mask and white-noise machine Charlie had purloined from Guest Services obscuring the day manager's footfalls. A suite of embarrassments followed: the older woman he'd met at a bar in Greenwich Village forcibly asking him to leave her apartment when she returned early from a trip to Paris, angry that he'd let himself back in, after they'd said their good-byes, by tricking her aging doorman; being rousted by the Pakistani teenager whose bed he'd stolen at the Big Apple Hostel in Times Square; the waitress threatening to call the police if he didn't pay up and leave; the security guard discovering him camped out in the accidentally unlocked first-editions room of the New York Public Library.

The miracle that stabilized his living situation first appeared to him a mirage. A heat-induced chimera in Shelleyan's likeness sauntered down Minetta Lane one particularly airless afternoon, checking her hair in the reflection of the Black Rabbit, a wood-paneled bar on the corner.

Charlie peered at her, overtaken by serendipity. Surely her presence was an omen that he was treading the right path, that the hazy journey from Arizona to Vermont to New York would bring him back to Olivia. He straightened his back, shifting his dirty duffel bag to obscure his meager possessions. Perhaps Shelleyan would even act as the conduit.

"It is you!" Shelleyan cried. "I thought it was. How are you?" She looked exactly the same, as if the Arizona Shelleyan had a twin living in New York City, save for the stylish haircut that gave her the air of working in an office.

"Fine," he answered, "I'm fine." She lunged at him for a quick hug. "I've been in Vermont."

"What have you been doing in Vermont?" she asked.

"Studying writing at Camden," he said, baiting her. Would she remember Camden as the school Downs had made famous? He regretted it instantly, the scene where Shelleyan taunted him about his ignorance of Olivia's penchant for the works of Vernon Downs was still fresh. If she asked him what he was working on, or what he'd written, he knew he'd blank, incapable of even devising a fake title to offer as proof of his new phantom identity.

Shelleyan nodded. The clue eluded her, which convinced him that what she had professed to know about Vernon Downs she'd aped from

Olivia's interest only to harangue him, and he hated her for it anew.

"What are you doing here?" he asked.

"I live here," she answered.

"Where?" he asked. Had she seen him living on the streets, working up the courage to approach him, maybe at Olivia's insistence, from whatever safe roof housed her?

"Williamsburg," she told him. "Or East Manhattan, as we say in Billyburg."

Charlie was baffled by what she was talking about, but nodded nonetheless.

"I transferred to Parsons," she continued. "Where are you staying?"

"East Village," he lied. It was the only neighborhood he could convincingly speak of.

"Very cool," Shelleyan said.

A cab lurched down the lane and they both watched as it rolled to a stop at the entrance to the shuttered Minetta Lane Theatre. An athletic cabbie with shoulder-length hair braided against the heat shook the locked theater doors and then drove off.

"Have you heard from Olivia?" she asked, as if intuiting the thought that had dried on his lips.

His nerves jangled at the sound of her name. He felt the sudden need to confide his ploy to impress Olivia with his connection to Vernon Downs, but all there was to disclose was his objective and its unsuccessful execution. "You guys stay in touch?" He winced as the question landed. The answer would tell him how much she knew about what had been said between them during that last phone call.

"She doesn't have my new address," Shelleyan admitted. "I need to write her."

Charlie clenched his bag. "Sounds like a plan," he said, baffled at why Shelleyan had engaged him in such friendly conversation, if not at Olivia's bidding. The concept that he and Shelleyan would be friends so far from home seemed improbable. Their roles had been cast back in Phoenix, their relationship previously defined. "Hey, I've got to run. I'm meeting someone. . . ." He motioned in the direction of the Black Rabbit.

"Is this your regular?" she asked, appraising the bar.

"It's just a bar," he said. "Great to see you."

"Okay," Shelleyan said, and he rushed past her, touching her on the shoulder to evade the good-bye hug he sensed was imminent. "Wait!"

He turned around, his dirty duffel swinging violently.

"Let me get your number." She rummaged in her bag. "Be fun to have old home week, huh?"

The open door to the Black Rabbit was less than fifty feet away. "You can always reach me here," he said, jamming his thumb at the gold-stenciled window. He laughed to indicate it might be a joke and it might not, waving and disappearing into the dark, cool bar. He spied Shelleyan copying the phone number into her address book. The sight of her provoked a set of fragile emotions: On the one hand, a sense of welcome familiarity gripped him, as if he and Shelleyan and Olivia had lunched together in the Milky Way yesterday rather than forever ago; but all that had happened to him since reminded him that Olivia, too, was off somewhere living her life while he was absent from her life. He longed to staunch the accumulation of time spent apart, and Shelleyan's presence was a further insult to his situation.

Charlie watched from the safety of a dim corner until Shelleyan was lost in a sea of NYU kids migrating toward Sixth Avenue. The empty bar had the clean smell of freshly polished wood. The elderly bartender nattily attired in a pressed white cotton shirt and vintage gold vest busied himself with aligning the bottles of liquor behind the bar, rotating the labels face out, putting his eyes in the mirror only when Charlie turned to leave.

"Drink?" the bartender asked. A streak of late-afternoon light lit a dust mote that floated aflame across the vacant bar.

Charlie hesitated. He knew that wood-paneled bars like the Black

Rabbit were generally more expensive than the sinkholes on the Lower East Side—he'd wandered into the Oak Room at the Plaza Hotel after an afternoon idle in Central Park and was dismayed at the fifty-dollar check for two vodka tonics and a watercress sandwich. He hadn't even known what watercress was, and while he enjoyed the sandwich, he would forever associate it with that afternoon's extortion.

"Maybe a glass of water," Charlie answered, "if you can spare it."

The bartender smiled. "You look like you need something a little stronger than water."

Charlie pulled out a barstool, convinced that this old man was going to sucker him by selling him a drink he needed but couldn't afford. His insides were still electrified from Shelleyan's unforeseen appearance, and the fortitude he needed to endure the harsh conditions on the streets of New York had momentarily been flushed from his system.

The bartender poured a tall, frosty glass of amber ale and set it in front of him. "On the house," he said without fanfare.

A store of self-pity welled up and it was all he could do to refrain from leaping over the bar to hug the bartender, or to curb the tears tickling the corners of his eyes. He lifted the glass in the bartender's direction. "Cheers," he said, the first taste of the cold beer going down a little too easily.

The bartender gave his name, and Charlie listened as Frank related how he'd once been a Broadway producer, "back when New York was New York," telling about the theater he had called home and all the wonderful friends who were long gone. "Some of them are on the wall," he said, indicating the framed pen and pencil caricatures that lined the establishment. Frank poured Charlie another beer, then one for himself. "What do you do?" he asked.

"I'm a writer," Charlie said, sipping the fresh beer.

"What have you written?" Frank asked.

Charlie babbled an unintelligible monologue about a novel that too closely resembled the mashed-up plots of two of Vernon Downs's novels, and he hoped that Frank wasn't a rabid Downs fan. "So far unpublished," he added quickly.

"Just takes luck," Frank said. "So many people in the theater had the most amazing stories about finding fortune. Some owed their whole career to standing in the right spot at the right time." He raised his glass. "To luck."

Charlie lifted his half-full glass. "To luck," he repeated.

Frank drained his glass and quickly washed it in the bar sink, replacing the sparkling pint on the pyramid of glasses behind the bar. "My friend owns a small publishing house in Brooklyn," Frank said. "You should send him your book."

Frank's mounting kindness toward him washed away all of Charlie's anxieties, and he deeply wished the imaginary manuscript existed, if only to repay the charity that Charlie knew he didn't deserve. He pocketed the address Frank scrawled on a cocktail napkin bearing a foil silhouette of a small black rabbit.

It was a number of days before Charlie learned that Obelisk Press was in the Williamsburg neighborhood in Brooklyn, the same neighborhood where Shelleyan lived, and the notion of paying a visit—he was slowly learning that every connection in New York deserved tribute—gave him the heebie-jeebies. Accident brought him to the crumbling concrete steps of the gray building in the Puerto Rican section of Williamsburg one Wednesday afternoon: He was enjoying an afternoon getaway from the city courtesy of a flyer he'd found in the subway advertising a kickball tournament in McCarren Park, in Greenpoint, the neighborhood abutting Williamsburg. As the sun set on the kickballers, Charlie trudged back toward the subway, his stomach full from the free hot dogs and watery beer served to spectators and players alike by the Turkey's Nest, a dive bar that was also the tournament's sole sponsor. An adventurous jaunt down a quiet side street designed to prolong the redemptive afternoon led him instead to the discreet plaque advertising the publishing company Frank had steered him and his imaginary manuscript toward.

He knocked on the door, unsure what he'd say. No one answered. He knocked again, spying the buzzer at knee height. He bent down, his back aching from leaning or lying on the grass all day, and pressed the buzzer. The front door was jimmied open by an enormous man in his sixties dressed in an impeccable three-piece suit, a neatly trimmed white beard the only hair on his pink head. Charlie introduced himself as a friend of Frank's. He didn't know Frank's last name, and Frank had only suggested mailing his imaginary manuscript, not showing up at the address in Brooklyn, but Charlie's instinct was stronger than reason and always prevailed. The man was searching Charlie's face, trying to fathom what it was he was saying, when Charlie remembered the folded napkin in his wallet. He offered the napkin with Frank's scrawl and the man's eyes lit up. He hoped Frank wouldn't learn of this misapplication of his kindness, though he was fairly sure he would never see Frank again, or could avoid him if it became an issue, so he dispatched the worry as quickly as it arose.

"Ah, yes," he said. "Come in."

The man introduced himself as Derwin MacDonald, though his affiliation with Frank from the Black Rabbit was to be forever unknown. Obelisk Press occupied the entire first floor of the building, the second being Derwin's living quarters. Charlie accepted Derwin's offer of a strong cup of coffee and, grateful for a comfortable chair, settled into the low-lit living room as Derwin recounted his days as a hanger-on in London, on the fringes of the third incarnation of the Bloomsbury Group, which Derwin explained was a group of intellectuals, writers, and painters. He glossed over the group's demise owing to vanity and fervent self-publication, Obelisk rising from the ashes of the immolation to publish the writers and thinkers he admired most.

"Do you write?" Derwin asked.

"I'd like to be a writer," Charlie admitted.

"Ah," Derwin said. "That's not the same thing."

Charlie shrugged and peppered him with questions about London, what it was like to live there, how expensive it was compared with New York, what single people did for fun, etc., keeping silent on the nature of his inquiry. He was dismayed at the glorious portrait Derwin painted, worried that Olivia might realize that she was already living in one of the most desirable world capitals and lose any interest in returning to America, for any reason.

By the end of the evening, he felt as integrated as he had since he'd left Phoenix, and by the end of the week he was squatting in the tiny studio apartment on the third floor, above Obelisk Press, with Derwin's permission. A foldout couch sat unevenly on the hardwood floor next to a table with spindly legs piled high with copies of Obelisk titles. A small counter installed under the far eave supported a toaster and a defunct coffeemaker. What he mistook for a closet was actually a half bathroom. The room suited him fine. He'd long ago given up trying to personalize any of the spaces he inhabited.

His apprehension at bumping into Shelleyan on the streets of Williamsburg faded as he acclimated to his new lodgings, and when Derwin offered him a part-time job as his right-hand man, he felt landed enough to call Vernon Downs, whose number he still knew by heart.

....

As he knocked on Downs's door, Charlie was revisited by an old humiliation from his first week in New York. Fearing that he'd be chased from the city and never have the chance, he had managed a call to Downs. Their staccato conversation—mostly Charlie giving a nervous recitation about what had transpired after his public reading of Downs's work—was cut short with a proffered invitation, a book party at the National Arts Club in Gramercy Park. Charlie thanked him profusely, and Vernon said he was looking forward to meeting then, which provoked a crippling anxiety that lasted until the party. It was some small relief, then, when the doorman at the National Arts Club forbade him entrance for lack of a jacket.

"Gentlemen wear jackets," the doorman snobbishly suggested. The snub ignited Charlie's inclination toward flight, which he'd felt when he first arrived at the Kepharts', and the McCallahans', and the Alexander-Degners'—on down the line. Over the years, he'd noticed a tickle when inaugurated into a new situation, one that implored him to turn back, or to press on quickly. He fought against the feeling but bailed from the foyer as the doorman hunted up a club jacket for him to wear. An aggregate of humiliation could only lead to certain ruin. But would Vernon remember Charlie standing him up? Or worse, had he somehow witnessed his humiliation as the doorman shook his head sternly, like the nannies did their charges in Gramercy Park on the sunny days since that Charlie had spent canvassing the scene of the crime, the interior of the National Arts Club a mystery still? He had considered calling Vernon the next day and leaving a cheery message saying he'd see him later that night, pretending to be mistaken about the date, ultimately glad that he hadn't. One of the dilemmas about an uncertain present was an indecipherable future.

He'd had to invent a pretext for a second call, especially after his unexplained National Arts Club absence, and he manufactured an assignment he hadn't been given: He asked Vernon if he could interview him for *Oneironaut*, an online pop culture magazine whose founder he'd befriended in line at Starbucks.

"Sure," Vernon had said. "Be happy to."

The door opened slowly, a pair of cautious eyes peering from behind it. The door opened further and Vernon Downs stood before him, a tall, bulky man in his midthirties, a half smile on his cherubic face, the living embodiment of the description from the *Vanity Fair* profile he and Olivia had read repeatedly. A slight embarrassment passed between them.

"Come in," he said, his baritone voice filling the cavernous loft as Charlie entered.

II

"FOR OLIVIA?" Vernon asked.

Charlie nodded as he fished the tattered copy of *The Vegetable King* Olivia had left behind from his bag.

"This looks pretty beat up," Vernon said, fanning through the curled pages. "I think I can do better." He slid back the doors on the white and maple sideboard table packed with books and, not finding what he was searching for, reached under the unmade bed for a plastic bin crammed with copies of his work. He selected a pristine copy of *The Vegetable King* and signed it to Olivia. He signed the worn copy too, splaying the book out on the black granite kitchen counter, the only shadow anywhere in the gleaming white loft. "You can sell this one for a couple of bucks at the Strand." Charlie nodded, remembering the mammoth bookstore on Twelfth Street from when he'd cased Vernon's block upon learning Vernon's address.

The light outside the oversized windows was fading, a dusky glow painting the white walls gold. The stainless steel fan Vernon had switched on during the interview rotated, its blades flashing, the breeze rippling the cloth folding screen in the opposite corner that sequestered a table and computer. Vernon flicked on the track lighting and the loft, which had previously felt like a theater stage, took on the warmth of a habitable apartment. Charlie's anxiety at meeting Vernon had dissipated over the course of the interview, and he had become captivated by Vernon's answers, querying him exhaustively with the ambition of knowing every nuance about the author and his life. In the span of an afternoon, he'd become the world's expert on all things Vernon Downs, and for a brief moment he wished to time-travel back to the Milky Way Café at Glendale Community College so that instead of uttering "Why do I know that name?" he could proclaim "Of course, Vernon Downs."

"I'll ride down with you," Vernon said as he stabbed his cigarette into the pewter ashtray engraved with WORLD'S GREATEST DAD, which had slowly filled during the interview. Vernon cradled the ashtray and moved them into the elevator with a jauntiness that belied what must've been the incredible stress of the last couple of months. His smooth face was unblemished and he projected a vigor Charlie associated with health spas and resort living and not virtual exile in a small loft in New York City. "Be sure to show me the interview before you send it," he said. "Just to make sure I didn't say anything, you know, ridiculous."

Charlie promised he would. The elevator opened on the second floor just as Vernon said, "I'm having a little party," and Charlie was too exhilarated at the invitation to Vernon's famous annual Christmas in July party to really register Vernon's scattering the remnants from his ashtray in the hall, the heaviest concentration of butts littering the doorway of apartment 2D. Vernon stepped back into the elevator and it completed its descent to the lobby. "You should definitely stop by."

Charlie suppressed his elation. "I will," he said, "thanks a lot," regretting the "a lot" as soon as it left his mouth. The division between those on the inside and those on the outside was just circumstance and chance, he thought.

"And I'd love to see some of your work." Vernon slipped the ashtray into the back pocket of his black jeans.

"Oh," Charlie said, more in surprise than in response to the enormous gratitude the gesture inspired. He shifted into the rote supplication he could conjure at will while he considered what work he could show. He had his Oswald story, but he'd also managed to finish the story loosely based on him and Olivia for his Camden workshop. He'd feigned illness rather than attend workshop the day his story was to be discussed—he hadn't changed Olivia's name and understood too late that he wouldn't be able to weather others speaking about her in any way, even as a fictional character, so much so that he left the copies with his workshop mates' edits unread in a trash can in Booth before lighting out for New York. He was curious what Vernon would make of the story, though, and was also thrilled that he would soon be introduced to Olivia, albeit only on the page.

The genuineness of Vernon's invitation to the party and his offer to read some of Charlie's work caught Charlie off guard, and he exited the lobby before he could utter something foolish that might persuade Vernon otherwise, but Vernon was engrossed in conversation with the doorman, complaining of someone smoking in the halls. The doorman promised to investigate, and Charlie wondered what the gag was.

. . . .

In honor of the invitation to Vernon's party, Charlie bought a new shirt. He'd spent the afternoon at Century 21, the discount clothing store near Wall Street. Previously, his fashion sense had been limited to the rudimentary understanding most men held about colors that clashed. He had enlisted the help of the salesgirl, who smelled like vanilla, and he gave a start when the elevator to Vernon's loft opened on the second floor and a woman wearing the exact same scent emerged from apartment 2D. Charlie glanced guiltily at the carpeted hall, which had been recently vacuumed. He smiled at the woman, who was wearing a cornflower blue silk pleated dress that matched the color of her eyes.

He held the door for the woman and she disappeared into Vernon's party like quicksilver. Charlie maneuvered through the crowded loft with the manila envelope containing a copy of the story he'd written at

Camden. Trajectory after trajectory was aborted, guests crashing into him as he sought out his host, who was sequestered in the corner with the rented sound system that rendered conversation in the loft impossible. As he cut through the crowd, he found himself next to an actress he recognized from one of Olivia's favorite movies. The actress was drunk, relying on the nearest blank wall to keep her upright. He surveyed the loft and realized the party was peopled with celebrities. The lead singer of a band he had worshipped one summer in high school was chatting up Vernon, and Charlie stalled his approach.

Vernon waved him over.

"Thanks again for inviting me," Charlie said, awkwardly sticking out his hand, as if they hadn't previously met. In one unbroken gesture, Vernon shook his hand and introduced him to the lead singer, whose name he couldn't hear over the blaring music but knew nonetheless. "I brought a story," Charlie said, offering up the envelope, intuiting just then that it was completely the wrong venue and occasion to pass work to Vernon. Vernon responded by gracefully nodding and taking the envelope, slipping it behind one of the speakers. The hardwood floor was littered with silver and gold confetti, and a bodybuilder in a Santa suit hoisting a tray of hors d'oeuvres slipped and fell, scattering his payload, though hardly anyone noticed.

Charlie felt like a child who had strayed into a parental gathering, past his bedtime, and excused himself on the pretense of getting a drink. "Can I get you anything?" he asked Vernon, regretting this sycophancy, but Vernon didn't hear—or pretended not to—and Charlie slunk away, inching through the mob toward the makeshift bar. He felt a hand squeeze his arm and turned to find himself latched to a woman with enormous red lips.

"Vernon!" the lips shouted, and then just as quickly, "Oh, I'm sorry."

"I'm Charlie," he said, but the woman was skimmed away by a tide of revelers.

The movie poster for *Minus Numbers* loomed over the bar, the actor who had played the lead pointing at the poster, his face betraying the years since the film's release, as he strove to convince a skeptical blond woman that he was the actor on the poster.

"It's really me," the actor argued, a drunken grin spreading across his face.

The blond woman rolled her eyes and departed the bar with her drink, nearly charging into Charlie, whom she looked past as she scrutinized the faces in the loft.

The bartender, a tall, tanned woman in a gauzy dress, cupped her ear as he shouted his drink order, nodding as she poured out the last swallow of a bottle of tonic. Jeremy Cyanin materialized at Charlie's side. In all but a handful of the gossip column accounts of Vernon's alleged antics in bars and nightclubs from the Lower East Side to the Hamptons, Cyanin had been implicated as Vernon's accomplice, the two often referenced in the same breath. Cyanin's first novel, *Fiesta!* was published to critical and popular success simultaneous to Vernon's *Minus Numbers*, and as both novels explored disaffected youth, the press rendered the two writers interchangeable and began confusing them in print regularly. Their author photos from the decade previous had been reprinted thousands of times, so that the casual reader couldn't tell them apart, or recognize them now. Cyanin's reputation had been enhanced by a short stint as an ambulance driver during the first Gulf War—though a leg injury had deposited him safely stateside, where he continued his job as a fact-checker for the *New Yorker*—and from his surviving a small-plane crash during an African safari he'd taken with his first wife. (Cyanin had been married multiple times, each marriage beginning on the heels of the last.) The couple had been rescued by a passing sightseeing bus, only to have their second plane crash. Cyanin had suffered a ruptured spleen, a sprained arm, smashed vertebrae, a burned scalp, and a transitory loss of all feeling in his hands. To his eternal amusement, he had been declared dead and read his own obituary in a café in Venice, a fact he often mentioned in interviews.

"Another," he said to the bartender.

"One sec," the bartender said, holding up a finger as she turned to rummage through the cardboard boxes of unopened bottles of gin, tequila, vodka, whiskey, and rum.

Charlie grasped for something to say to Cyanin, but his thoughts were hijacked by the memory of Vernon referring to Cyanin as obsequious when Charlie tried to initiate small talk while waiting for the elevator. "He's still an obsequious presence at nightclubs." Vernon had meant "ubiquitous." The malapropism had plagued him, a catch in his throat that surfaced as he stood side by side with Cyanin. To his relief, Cyanin paid him no attention, staring straight ahead until a murderous shriek broke his trance. A woman grabbed Cyanin and kissed him on the lips. Cyanin pulled back, pretending offense.

"Is that a promise or a reprimand?" he asked, oozing a phony charm.

The woman hiccupped loudly and then proceeded not to be embarrassed when it was discovered that she'd mistaken Cyanin for her ex-husband, a bond trader for Salomon Brothers. "You actually don't look a thing like him," she said.

"He's a very lucky man," Cyanin said, swiping his fresh drink from the bar without breaking conversation. Charlie grabbed his vodka tonic as well, pointedly thanking the bartender, and turned away from Cyanin to face a platoon of thirsty partygoers impatiently questing for another drink.

"I loved your book," a bespectacled man said.

"Excuse me?" Charlie said. The vodka began massaging his brain.

"I said I loved your book," the man repeated, the scent of whiskey on his breath. Charlie noticed the man teetering slightly in his tasseled loafers. "I thought the characterizations were . . . real and the story . . . believable," the man said.

Charlie smiled, nodding as the man continued to praise whatever book he was referring to.

"Is it hard to write a book like that?" the man asked.

"Yes," Charlie said. "Very hard. Harder than you'd think."

"I'm Peter Kline," the man said. "I'm with the *Times*."

Charlie suspected Kline wouldn't remember the conversation and indulged him, grateful for someone to talk to.

"What I really liked was the way you couldn't tell if the main character—what was his name again?" Kline exhaled a stream of sour breath as he fumbled.

"I'm sorry," Charlie said. "I'm deaf in one ear. What did you say?"

"The main character in *The Vegetable King*," Kline said. "His name is escaping me."

"Nick Banks," Charlie said.

"I liked the way you couldn't tell if Nick Banks was really doing those murders, or if they were all just his imagination," Kline said.

Charlie sipped his drink, annoyed. "You couldn't tell? Thought it was obvious."

Kline didn't register the barb. "This is some party," he said. "Lots of celebs. Saw you with Jeremy Cyanin over there by the bar. Your partner in crime, eh?" Kline winked conspiratorially. "He says you don't like your picture taken."

Charlie smiled sheepishly. "Just doesn't seem like a good idea," he said. The cadence of Vernon's speech had been indelibly recorded in Charlie's brain, and he contorted his mouth to imitate the smirk he'd seen Vernon employ when he'd asked him the same question.

Kline winked again, making a gun with his fingers. "Gotcha. Lots of nut jobs out there." The commotion around a handstand by an attractive woman whose dress gathered down around her shoulders obscured Kline's good-bye as he joined the tributary of people moving slowly toward the balcony. Charlie swayed with the crowd until Kline was gone and then made his way for the door. He'd stayed long enough to recount the party to Olivia and glanced toward Vernon, hoping to give a salute across the noisy room, but Vernon was still in the corner, the woman with the cornflower blue dress whispering into his ear. He laughed and she leaned her body into his.

A boisterous foursome burst into the lobby, late arrivals for the party raging upstairs. Charlie lingered, eavesdropping on their excited chatter about meeting Vernon Downs, before catapulting out into the night, his senses ablaze with a privileged glimpse of the world Olivia must've dreamed of a thousand times over.

....

Charlie announced himself to the doorman, who registered a faint look of recognition. The doorman hung up the phone. "He's coming down." Charlie had almost missed the message Vernon had left the day before at Obelisk, asking him to join him for lunch. He had spent most of the previous day uptown with Derwin, who had arranged a launch party for Jacqueline Turner, one of his oldest authors, at Bemelmans in the Carlyle Hotel. Derwin had advanced him his paycheck so he could buy a suit for the occasion, again with the assistance of the vanilla-laced salesgirl at Century 21, who remembered him, or pretended to. New York's reputation as a cold, heartless metropolis was unearned, in his judgment. Eastern Star, the former speakeasy on the same block as Obelisk, had become Charlie's local, and he was amazed at the disparate population he'd encountered at the Star's lacquered and pockmarked bar: faces from Florida and Texas and Oregon, or Canada and Europe and Asia—each as friendly as the last, always inquiring what had brought Charlie to New York. He always demurred and instead luxuriated in their answers to the same question, drinking in the various biographies and ambitions. The Vietnamese girl who was studying fashion at Pratt; the Australian couple who hoped to open an apiary somewhere in Brooklyn; the kid from

Detroit who had dreams of becoming a hatter. Their ambitions were end-less and Charlie lamented only that he'd never know if any or all of them would come to fruition.

Charlie's stomach gurgled, reproof that he hadn't eaten since the Southern-themed launch party at Bemelmans the day before. The plate of leftover pecan-encrusted sliced chicken breast drizzled in honey and red-skinned mashed potatoes he'd wolfed down was a distant culinary event, and he hoped Vernon's plans for lunch were more than liquid. Jacqueline Turner had abstained from the delicious fare at her launch party, which Charlie ascribed to nerves. Leading up to the party, Derwin had been distracted with the details. What was left unsaid was that with Jacqueline being eighty, this would surely be her last novel, and even Derwin knew that it would not be remembered or read in the future. Charlie wondered if the same was true for her first novel, *Esque*. A framed enlargement of the cover hung over Derwin's desk, the author photo a stunning portrait of Jacqueline in her youth, her even features lending her an aura of grace. The knowing eyes bored out from the frame as Charlie considered the art deco design on the cover. The novel had won several of the major fiction prizes the year it was published, and Jacqueline had written two more in short order that sold well enough to her new audience, which thinned with each subsequent title, until she stopped publishing altogether at the young age of forty. Charlie bristled at the notion that it was possible to go from gracing the cover of *Time* magazine to obscurity within the same lifetime. Vernon Downs would be famous his entire life, probably post-humously, too. Jacqueline's death would merit an obituary in the *New York Times*, and Derwin would keep her work in print as long as he was alive, but it would probably suffer the miserable fate of being stacked in warehouses waiting for readers whose attention had turned elsewhere. The launch party for Jacqueline's new novel—sparsely attended by friends of Derwin's as well as a smattering of Jacqueline's contemporaries, and none of the press outlets Derwin had Charlie fax his carefully worded press release to—telegraphed just such ignominy. Charlie had helped himself to seconds after the small gathering had cleared, the caterer's assistant eyeing the same prize. Charlie knew the hunger with which free food was devoured, and he imagined the assistant would be lunching on pecan-encrusted chicken sandwiches for weeks.

"Sorry, sorry," Vernon said as he hustled into the lobby. "I have to go uptown."

A black sedan Charlie hadn't previously noticed idled out in front of Summit Terrace. His hunger rose up against his inclination toward genuflection but was defeated. "No problem, really."

"Ride with me," Vernon said. "I read your story."

The driver opened the door for Vernon and grimaced as Charlie skirted around to the other side, never having had a car door opened on his behalf. The leather interior was remarkably hard, and Charlie bounced in his seat as the car turned uptown, sailing up Park Avenue South. The landscape transformed dramatically as they sluiced through the tunnels at Grand Central, awash in the gilded moraine of centuries of wealth accumulation. Across Park Avenue, across the wide boulevard of landscaped tulips, a silver Jaguar gleamed heroically in a showroom window.

The interim between Charlie's handing over his story to now had been teeming with grand designs of becoming Vernon's protégé, fêted up and down Manhattan as the Next Big Thing, perhaps replacing the dull, aging Cyanin as Vernon's literary yin. If simply knowing Vernon was currency in Olivia's eyes, his becoming a protégé would make him richer by ten. The fantasies about celebrity-studded book parties and lucrative film offers were brought low now that he was cocooned in the sedan with Vernon. Charlie hadn't done more than transcribe his and Olivia's story, the pages likely rotten with florid language as a result of the seismic ache in his heart. That Vernon Downs would be remotely intrigued by the story suddenly seemed a severe miscalculation.

"I read it twice," Vernon said, tapping his slender fingers on the arm-rest between them. "You're onto something, but it's not happening on the page yet. Nothing happens, for one. Characters need backstory, but Alice is down the rabbit hole on page one, if you get me. And action is borne from motivation. So for instance, the girlfriend doesn't just move back home. They're engaged and she breaks up with him to marry someone else. But even that is too boring. She marries the other guy because the other guy has money, which is important because the girlfriend's family fortunes are dwindling. Maybe the result of scandal. Etcetera."

Charlie swallowed the revulsion he felt at the idea of Olivia marrying someone else, or marrying someone else for money. The offense was too grievous to consider, even fictionally. Vernon's advice called to mind those critics who had wondered where the emotional heft was in his work, complaining that his novels were too often peopled with ciphers meant to channel the author's ennui. One particular critic had called Vernon's work "everythingless."

Charlie mentally argued against Vernon's critique but was distracted by Vernon adding, casually, "I think I know an editor who would consider it if you revise." The hard truth that he needed Vernon's approval, craved the apprenticeship, stifled all his argumentative impulses.

"I'll definitely have another go at it," he said. "Thanks. Really, thanks."

"Pull over here," Vernon told the driver. The car found the nearest curb and Vernon turned in his seat. "Here's how you can return the favor." The directness of his tone spooked Charlie and he was taken aback by the cold fear he felt. He hadn't previously considered Vernon to be dangerous, but even the driver averted his eyes. "Write me five hundred words on why kids are ruining America."

"You mean like an essay?" Charlie asked, laughing.

Vernon smiled, clenching and unclenching his fists as if the reps were part of a daily exercise routine. "It's for *George* magazine. I told them I'd do it, but that was only because I wanted to meet JFK Jr. I'm just not into it now." He searched Charlie's face for complicity. "Do this for me and I'll show your story to my friend the editor."

Charlie nodded, knowing the hunger for ingratiation. "Sure. When do you need it?"

"Yesterday." Vernon grimaced. "Why don't you bring it with you to KGB tomorrow night. There's a book party. Seven p.m."

"Okay," Charlie agreed. It was easy to agree without considering what he was agreeing to.

"This is you," Vernon said. It took Charlie a moment to realize what Vernon was saying.

"Watch traffic," the driver warned from the front seat.

"Sorry about lunch," Vernon said.

Charlie waved good-bye and walked up Sixty-eighth Street, irresolute about the direction he was headed until Central Park came into view, orienting him. He was lost as a tourist uptown—his second trip in as many days—and almost collapsed in frustration until the doorman at the Plaza indicated with a nod the direction of the subway entrance under the hotel.

Charlie mounted the steep stairs to KGB, emerging at the tiny second-floor bar whose walls were lined with Soviet memorabilia, framed posters of Stalin and Lenin and other unnamed politburo chiefs menacing the crowd of oblivious hipsters from above. He spotted Vernon under a poster of Yuri Andropov. As he knifed through the throng, he spied Jeremy Cyanin behind a near-life-size black-and-white head shot of the author whose books were stacked on the corner of the bar.

Charlie crept forward. He'd been confused by the lack of real instructions for delivering the *George* magazine piece—he surmised that Vernon hadn't asked him to e-mail it to avoid an electronic paper trail—and felt foolish for bringing it to the book party, even if those were Vernon's instructions. He'd nearly abandoned the assignment, unable to

come up with a slant that seemed worthy of a slick magazine, until he'd
solicited Derwin for his assessment of youth culture. Derwin had given
him a soulful look. "Murderers, rapists, gamblers," he'd said. "You never
heard of these things when I was young." Charlie had no independent
knowledge about whether the comparison was true or not, but once he
embraced Derwin's point of view, the piece flowed quickly:

> Teens are running roughshod over this country—murdering, raping, gam-
> bling away the nation's future—and we have bills for counseling and prison
> to prove it. Sure, not all kids are bad—but collectively, they're getting worse.
> Why should we blame ourselves? Things have changed drastically in the last
> twenty years, to the point where one can really only chuckle in grim dis-
> belief. Cheating on exams? Smoking cigarettes? Shoplifting? You wish.
> Murder, rape, robbery, vandalism: The overwhelming majority of these crimes
> are committed by people under twenty-five, and the rate is escalating rapidly.

He'd gone to sleep feeling mentally fatigued, spent from rearranging
sentences and auditioning words and phrases, searching for artistic expression of his borrowed idea, but also from the charge of aping Vernon's
cool attitude.

Vernon nodded in his direction, calling him over.

"You made it," Vernon said.

Charlie made a nervous joke about having gotten lost, even though
he hadn't.

"This is Jeremy Cyanin," Vernon said, pointing.

"Hey," Cyanin said coolly, scanning the room. "I suppose you're mad
at Vernon too."

Charlie smiled dumbly, unsure what the gibe meant, forcing Vernon
to explain that he'd been spending time with some models as research for
his next novel and had even participated in a photo shoot, but changed
his mind about signing the release form. Apparently, everyone was angry

about it, much to Cyanin's amusement. Charlie processed the information in the uncomfortable silence, which was broken by a woman dripping in gold lamé who squealed when she saw Vernon and Cyanin. "It *is* you," the woman said, raising her arms to allow the writers to hug her. Cyanin obliged, while Vernon lifted his glass in the woman's direction. "Hello, Vernon," she said. "I haven't seen you since your Christmas party. You never did say where you hired those elves from."

"The elves were two years ago," Cyanin said, laughing. He rocked back on his heels, unaware of the swaying.

The woman's expression changed. "Yes, I'm on some sort of blacklist, apparently." Vernon shrugged and rattled the ice in his glass. A cloud settled over the woman, whose gold lamé dress appeared rusty in the red-lit room.

Cyanin leaned into the bar, and Charlie passed the folded pages to Vernon, who slipped them into his suit jacket pocket with a half smile.

"Looks like a rip-off of *Minus Numbers*," Charlie said, indicating the blowup of the cover.

"You could say that," Vernon laughed.

The writer being celebrated appeared, a jaunty kid wearing a very authorial jacket, complete with elbow patches, and shook hands with Vernon as Cyanin emerged from the bar. Charlie exploited the seam created by Cyanin and reached out for the lip of the bar to pulley himself to the front of the crowd.

"That's a slick move," the man standing next to him said.

"Thanks," Charlie replied.

"If you can get the bartender's attention, you'll really have done it." He stuck out his hand. "Warren Thomas."

Charlie shook hands. "Your name sounds familiar," he said, having recently realized this was the correct thing to say in writerly circles.

"I write for *Esquire*," he said. "With Josh." He indicated the author whose book had brought them all together.

"Right," Charlie said, reaching into the recesses of his mind to seize the elusive strand that incorporated what he knew about Warren Thomas. The information bobbed up like a sunken piece of driftwood finally freed. "You wrote 'The Case for Vernon David Downs,'" right?"

Warren nodded. "Good recall."

Charlie gushed about how Warren's piece about the *Vegetable King* controversy had clearly been written by someone with a cool head, not someone caught up in the rhetoric and the heated moment. "He's here," Charlie said.

"Yeah, I saw him." Warren attempted to flag down the bartender, without success. "I heard he's finally crawling out of his cave. Good for him. A shitty way to have to live. I'd stand in the corner too, though. You never know who's out there."

"Do you think *The Vegetable King* is his best book? Or just the most famous?"

Warren finally reeled in the bartender, who didn't look up when Warren gave his order, then pointed at Charlie.

"Same," Charlie said.

Warren turned to him. "Truthfully, I think he's a sensationalist hack with a gift for self-promotion. That piece was assigned to me and I wrote it. But it was mental torture. I didn't come up with the headline and never felt like I was making the case for anything, frankly. Just doing my job. I could make a case for him being a talentless douche bag. Easily."

The bartender splashed the vodka tonics down on the bar. Charlie tipped a buck, like he'd seen others do, but the bartender didn't notice, and when Warren didn't follow, Charlie slipped the dollar back into his pocket.

Warren hoisted his glass and said, "Sorry to disappoint," before being swallowed up by the crowd, which had grown exponentially. Charlie cut a half-moon through the bodies to reach Vernon and Cyanin, who were in the corner, their backs to the crowd. A cumulus of cigarette smoke hung thickly overhead. The spiced fragrance of a clove cigarette filled his nose.

"Have some," Vernon said, palming a small chrome bullet into Charlie's hand. The tiny cylinder felt hot to his touch, and he instinctively set his drink on the nearest table and unscrewed the top. Charlie had never favored anything more than drink, but reading Vernon's work had been, among other things, a study in the usage of drug paraphernalia. He scooped a tiny pyramid of cocaine with the miniature spoon inside and held it under his right nostril, inhaling quickly. A searing sandstorm blasted across the back of his throat, and his tongue involuntarily clamped to the roof of his mouth. Heart palpitations drowned the whirring in his brain as he resumed possession of his vodka tonic.

Vernon skulked in the corner, his arms crossed, striking the same pose he had at the Christmas party. Cyanin never strayed from his side, his animation contrasting violently with Vernon's passivity. Charlie felt his spine straighten as the cocaine massaged his doubts and fears about winning Olivia back into confirmation that all would be well. Something within him vindicated all designs of his thinking, vanquishing the interior monologue that constantly reminded him that he knew nothing definitively and that his life was essentially a streak of guesses.

Josh, the celebrated author, ducked into the bathroom in the hall. An acrid odor assaulted Charlie as he followed. His field of vision narrowed. Josh was at the sink, dabbing his wet fingers through his black hair. The phoniness of the assortment of bracelets on his right wrist struck Charlie as pathetic. Josh peered at Charlie in the mirror and Charlie tipped his chin. "Great party," he said.

"Cool," Josh said. The bracelets jangled as his hands dropped to his sides.

"I liked your book," Charlie said.

Josh turned and edged against the sink to let Charlie pass. "Thanks, man."

Charlie's heart raced and he stifled a cackle. "I mean, I liked it when it was called *Minus Numbers*."

The author grimaced, squinting.

"Seems like a pretty poor imitation," Charlie continued. "Actually, truth be told, it looks like garbage. I'm surprised there isn't a stack in here to wipe your ass with." The words issued from his mouth like gunfire.

"You're entitled to your opinion," Josh said. He pivoted, but Charlie barred his exit.

"Oh, it's more than an opinion," Charlie sneered. "It's an established fact."

"Can I pass?"

"Fact," Charlie repeated.

"May I pass?" Josh asked again.

"Sure." Charlie acquiesced, stepping aside. "You can do anything you want," he said. "Except come up with your own ideas, apparently."

"Fuck you," Josh blurted out as he lurched out the door.

Charlie lunged at the sink, his pulse quickening until his vision was permeated with bright constellations. He pressed his forehead against the mirror and watched his eyeballs shimmy in their sockets. He drank ravenously from the rusted tap, splashing the cool water on his face. Back in the bar, Vernon and Cyanin were sitting at a table, drinking and smoking. Charlie took the steps two at a time until he reached the street, the humidity lashing his forehead with sweat. He made his way toward Union Square, traffic blurring around him. As he plummeted into the swampy subway station, an immense exhaustion overtook him and he clutched the rail. A young girl with a blond beehive hairdo asked him if he was okay, and he moved on without answering, thinking about the question.

....

Charlie realized that a pain he had mistakenly diagnosed as a sore throat was actually a bad tooth. He disregarded the throbbing until it prevented him from sleeping, finally giving in to the unbelievable fire in his jaw, seeking treatment at the New York University dental school on the advice of Derwin, who'd had a successful cleaning there at a fraction of the cost. "Not to fret," Derwin said. "The students are supervised by faculty."

The days leading up to Charlie's appointment, mostly spent in agony in his cramped and stuffy studio apartment above Obelisk typing up his interview with Vernon, passed slowly. When he finally breached the doors of the dental clinic, it was with a sense of hope. He waited patiently to be called onto the floor, a cavernous space as big as a gymnasium outfitted with dental chairs and dental equipment, shiny and new enough to assuage Charlie's fears that the school was nothing more than a chop shop. He was introduced to the student who would be attending to his dental needs, a Russian whose name he didn't catch. A bit of pantomiming couldn't elicit his name again, and Charlie finally surrendered to the Russian's entreaty for him to open wide.

After a few moments of prodding, the Russian brought him upright and motioned for Charlie to follow him. He draped the heavy apron over Charlie and pointed for him to take a seat in a metal booth. The Russian pressed a cardboard splint loaded with film into Charlie's gums until they bled, finally finding the position he wanted. The Russian aimed the arm of the X-ray machine at his cheek and scampered away. As Charlie anticipated the high-pitched squeal of the X-ray machine, he noted a smear of dried blood on the booth that almost made him faint.

The Russian managed the words "root canal" and Charlie nodded, glad to have the problem out in the open. The Russian bade Charlie to follow him back to a dental chair, and he was quickly surrounded by three other heads that began speaking rapid-fire Japanese into his open mouth. Charlie had somehow assented to a root canal, and the foursome was going to extract the root in his ailing tooth right then and there. He wanted to protest, but the pain radiating from his mouth persuaded him to give it a shot.

The Novocain injection put the operation on the right footing. *These guys really know what they're doing*, Charlie thought. He relaxed as best he could as the Russian drilled open his bad tooth. He knew from previous root canals that the next step would be to remove the infected pulp tissue, which would alleviate the agony. The drilling was endless, though, exciting the Japanese students, whose instructions in Japanese the Russian didn't seem to understand. Charlie could sense the Russian becoming flustered, until he raised his arms in surrender. The five of them sat in silence, catching their breath, while Charlie stared at yet another dried bloodstain, this one on the overhead lamp. After a moment, the Russian wanted a second chance, which turned into a third and a fourth try. An hour passed while he tried to get at the infected tissue, and finally a balding man in a lab coat, who Charlie later learned was the instructor assigned to walk the floor, banished the foursome to another torture assignment and quickly finished extracting the tissue. He cleaned out the root canal and sealed it with a temporary filling.

"You'll have to come back on another visit to continue the procedure," the instructor said gruffly. "Make an appointment on your way out."

Charlie stood at the checkout desk, shaken, while a student wearing headphones looked into a computer monitor, booking him for an appointment he knew he wouldn't keep.

"Something in your teeth?" Vernon asked over drinks at the Gramercy Park Hotel bar. The drink was in celebration of Vernon's victory in a legal matter involving a studio and a director who had stolen the premise of one of Vernon's early published short stories, and Charlie had shown up on time, hoping to disappear before the arrival of Cyanin and the rest of Vernon's cadre of friends.

"Had a root canal this morning," Charlie said without elaboration. He knew not to burden Vernon with his personal problems.

"I hope that means painkillers," Vernon said.

"Tylenol Three," Charlie replied.

"Sucker," Vernon said, flashing him a half smile.

Charlie expected Vernon to comment on his piece for *George* magazine, but Vernon gave no indication that he'd even read it. Maybe he'd read and tossed it, instructing his agent to cancel the contract. Entirely possible. His heavily revised short story could meet the same fate. After agonizing over the sacrilege, he accepted Vernon's challenge and portrayed the character based on Olivia in the unsympathetic light Vernon had suggested. The story was now the tale of an idealistic young romantic whose heart was maliciously broken. When the young romantic chases the object of his affections to Europe, she tells him she had an abortion and that she can never see him again. Back home, the young romantic runs into a mutual friend, who tells him that the abortion was just a story to get rid of him. The ending leaves ambiguous what the young romantic does next.

"I took your advice," Charlie said. "About my story, I mean."

Vernon drained his vodka. "Cool," he said, crunching a piece of ice. "E-mail it and I'll have a look."

As Vernon dictated his e-mail address, Charlie was astounded at the simplicity of the combination of letters and symbols. He'd idly speculated that Vernon's e-mail address would incorporate something from one of his books, a character's name or a character's favorite restaurant or bar. The realization that the address was an AOL account simply prefaced with Vernon's initials was stupefying. The relief for those panic-stricken weeks back in Phoenix when he was frantic to arrange lunch with Olivia and Vernon could've been puzzled out if he weren't always trying to be clever. Sometimes the answer was simple, not a code to be broken. "He's Olivia's favorite writer, dummy," Shelleyan had said. He wished his answer could've been, "I'll drop him an e-mail and see if he's up for lunch."

"Excuse me, Mr. Downs?" The impeccably groomed waiter with the shiny black ponytail approached. "This is against hotel policy, but I wondered if you might sign a book for me." He presented a copy of *The Vegetable King* from the waistband of his black apron. "I hope it's okay to ask."

Charlie said, "Possible to get another drink?" before Vernon cut him off with a smirk. "It's no problem." He commandeered Charlie's pen and signed the book while the waiter glared at Charlie.

"I truly appreciate it," the waiter said. "I'm a tremendous fan, going back to *Minus Numbers*."

"Thanks," Vernon said quietly, rolling the pen back to Charlie. "You're not going to sell it at the Strand, right?"

"No, never," the waiter said.

"Possible to get a couple more?" Charlie asked brusquely.

"Same?" the waiter asked Vernon pointedly.

Vernon nodded, turning to Charlie as the waiter sauntered away. "Quit abusing my fans," he laughed.

"Just thought it was uncool," Charlie said reflexively.

Vernon regarded him with an air of amusement. The chandelier overhead dimmed and the red velvet lounge shaded, casting his features in relief. Charlie knew he'd overstepped, and waited for a rebuke. Instead Vernon said, "Would you be up for some apartment sitting?"

....

A sharp pain flashed through Charlie's brain and he slumped against the pillow, rubbing his dry eyes. Yesterday's Post lay on the floor, open to the piece that had brought on the frenzy he hadn't fully been able to subdue:

Vernon Downs Evades History

Vernon Downs has always had a knack for getting press, but young writers looking to hitch their wagons to his publicity mule should look elsewhere. *The Vegetable King* author tells us he is refusing to cooperate with an oral biography of his life and work being written by Jonathan Erdahl. According to anonymous sources, Erdahl intends to interview such literary folk as David Gomez, Jeff Lawrence, and Jeremy Cyanin. So why won't Downs touch the project with a ten-foot pen? A friend of his tells us, "He just isn't in the mood." Well, we're sure Erdahl will dig up something.

Charlie had no idea who in the fuck Jonathan Erdahl was, but the crest of jealousy that crashed over him as he reread the article was disorienting. That Vernon had never mentioned him assured Charlie that this Erdahl was just one more wannabe, someone Vernon had vanquished by leaking a quote that was certainly devastating to the project. Erdahl was finished. He wouldn't be digging up anything of any interest to anyone anytime soon.

The faded blue iguana stamped onto his left hand brought the previous night into focus, the no-name club where he ended up with Stacey, the woman he'd met at Bull & Bear, the restaurant at the Waldorf Astoria, who claimed to work for some sort of design company. He'd gone to Bull & Bear to remind himself that he could act like a gentleman, quietly sipping a Ketel One martini at the elegant bar while the youngish pianist played indistinct classical music. The cigar smoker in the suit might've assumed he was an investment banker, someone who lived uptown or off Central Park, or one of those computer gazillionaires who might be in from California to broker a deal. For the first time since he'd moved to New York, Charlie felt the pliant personality that had allowed him to move from town to town, home to home, school to school, emerge, and when Stacey sat down beside him and ordered a vodka sour, he decided to enlist his old powers. He could do that. Slough off the heavy baggage he'd ferried from Phoenix, always concentrating on the high-wire act he was trying to orchestrate. He said hello and remembered what it was like to pretend. He had Stacey calling him James, he had her riding in a cab going downtown, he had her drinking bourbon straight up at the International on First Avenue.

Then she had him dancing in a club full of people in Soho. Everything was green, the walls, the lights, the liquor they drank out of plastic cups. "This isn't crème de menthe, is it?" Charlie asked, but Stacey didn't hear him and then she was gone, swept up in a wash of green. He slipped into the bathroom and vomited until the toilet bowl matched the rest of the decor, and then he glided out the front door.

Charlie rubbed his eyes again. He had the feeling that he was forgetting something, leaving something out, but he could not summon a picture of what had happened next. He looked at the inch-high green digits on his alarm clock. He had guessed it was around noon and was dismayed to read that it was nearing five o'clock. He snatched up a half-eaten bag of lime-flavored tortilla chips and sat on the end of his bed, crunching loudly, the tinge of salt and lime filling his mouth and throat, wondering the extent of the hit his credit card took during the previous evening's escapades. When he learned later that his Visa was maxed out, he bent it in half and then in half again and flushed the pieces down the toilet.

A survey of his closet revealed that Charlie hadn't done laundry in a while. Why couldn't he remember these crucial chores? Derwin had invited him to use the washer and dryer in the basement anytime he wished. Charlie slipped on a pair of jeans not too dirty to wear and pulled on his favorite black T-shirt. He took the stairs gingerly and meandered to what was quickly becoming his favorite neighborhood bar, Iona. The bartender, Ailish, was the incarnation of Talie, the girl in foster care at the Chandlers' in Phoenix that he'd been close to, and it amused him to watch the place fill with men—some from Manhattan—waiting for their chance to flirt with her.

"How are you, Charlie?" Ailish said from behind the narrow bar, the playground for so many late-night conversations and flirtations. The track lighting overhead cast shadows around her as she emptied the pint glasses out of the dishwasher.

"I'm okay," he said. "What's new?"

"Remember that song you were trying to think of the other night?" Ailish had been playing all '80s music, and a lyric he couldn't identify had popped into Charlie's head. Charlie had argued it was a band called Camouflage, but Ailish said for sure it wasn't, though she couldn't remember exactly who it was.

"It was Camouflage," Charlie said, smiling.

Ailish slapped the bar towel at him. "I told you it wasn't fucking Camouflage," she said. "It's Real Life." She put her arms up over her head in victory.

"Yeah," Charlie said. "Real Life covering Camouflage."

"Oh, give it up," she said.

"I think you owe me a drink, then."

"How is it you got the answer wrong and I owe *you* a drink?" She acted incredulous, and it was one of the things Charlie loved about her, how any small thing could become a good time.

"How about if I buy me one and then you buy me one?" he offered.

"That's a *much* better deal," she laughed, and poured him a pint of Bass, which was how it always started.

By eleven o'clock, Charlie had lost sight of Ailish, not knowing it would be the last time he ever saw her, that a death in her family would call her back to Dublin. He looked at the apartment building across the street. All the windows were dark. Everyone was out somewhere, having a good time, or having a shitty time, he thought. Living their lives, regardless. Derwin had gone out of town for the weekend to visit his brother in Baltimore. Charlie didn't want to be the only soul in the building, which was how he ended up in a cab with two girls who were afraid to take the subway from Brooklyn late at night. He asked them their names twice as the cab sped over the Williamsburg Bridge, and then the girls ignored him, sorry they'd offered him a ride (he had just stepped out for some air, but the way he looked at the cab made them think he wanted to share it). Charlie got out at Houston and Broadway and handed the girls a five-dollar bill. "Nice to meet you, Becky and Julie," he said. "Thanks for the ride."

"Sandy and Emily," one of them said as Charlie slammed the cab door.

Charlie parted the black curtain under a neon sign on the Lower East Side, and his eyes dilated in the dark bar. Two girls dressed in identical pink plastic dresses looked up from the sofa by the door, their faces obscured in darkness. Charlie waved as if he knew them, and they looked back at each other and continued their conversation.

An uneasy feeling came over him as he battled for space at the bar. Finally he planted himself on the long couch in the back room. He would trade every good thing in his future if only Olivia would appear, kiss him on the cheek, rest her head on his shoulder. His heart contracted and he gasped for breath, sure that he was about to die. Two short breaths and he exhaled deeply, the weight he'd felt lifting right as the waitress poked her head in.

"Vodka tonic, please," Charlie said. "Stoli."

A song that had been popular when Charlie lived in Santa Fe played loudly overhead, and by the time it was finished, two empty glasses were keeping each other company on the table near the couch as he recounted for Lynette—a girl who had come in looking for her friends, for a birthday party—the different meanings the song had held for him at different points in his life. Charlie was making a very moving point about his childhood when Lynette interrupted him to ask the difference between a Sea Breeze and a Bay Breeze. Charlie couldn't guess and said so. He put his head on Lynette's bare shoulder and she didn't seem to mind. He felt her body vibrate when she told the waitress, "Sea Breeze, please," and he started humming the song that had just ended. By the time he was in the cab with Lynette, headed to an Albanian nightclub Lynette knew about somewhere in the Bronx, Charlie was humming the tune for the cabdriver, asking if the cabbie knew the name of the song, or who sang it.

"I have to get up early," Lynette said to no one in particular. A mole on her neck would be unsightly once Lynette was older—she'd likely have it removed—but Charlie thought it was so sexy he wanted to lean in and kiss it.

"Where do you work?" Charlie asked, but he didn't listen to the answer.

The cab flew up Madison Avenue, the streets desolate except for the occasional couple strolling in front of backlit windows, peering in at chicly dressed mannequins wearing frozen expressions.

"Take us to Fifty-fifth and Fifth," Lynette yelled, leaning through the plastic divider. Charlie glimpsed a second beauty mark on her breast that mirrored the one on her neck, and he yearned to trace an arc between the two.

"Is that where you live?" Charlie asked.

"There's a cool bar," Lynette said, her thoughts drifting. "I went there once with my father."

The cab stopped on Fifth Avenue and Charlie paid the driver, then tipped the doorman at the Peninsula Hotel. Lynette pressed the button for the elevator, and Charlie slipped into the men's room, vomiting in a stall, bracing himself against the cold steel walls. He fixed his hair in the mirror, and the elevator rang as the men's room door closed behind him.

The bar on the roof of the Peninsula was unoccupied, and Charlie looked at his watch: 3:30. A light breeze swooped down and made him shiver.

"What are you drinking?" Lynette asked.

Charlie ordered a vodka and cranberry from the tuxedo-clad bartender. "We're closed after this," the bartender said, and brushed his crew cut.

"So are we," Charlie said, but no one laughed.

The cranberry juice tasted like food to Charlie as he slowly tilted his head back. He opened his eyes and spied the moon peeking through a jumble of clouds. He thought he could feel the light coming off the moon, not heat but a soothing coolness, like the water in the pool Lynette spotted on their way to the elevator, her dress already poolside by the time Charlie splashed down. Floating on his back, he was unsure if they'd paid for their drinks. He closed his tired eyes and put his hands at his sides and began to sink toward the bottom.

....

The doorman nodded at Charlie as he whisked through the lobby of Summit Terrace. He reflected on the progression of faces the doorman must log during the course of the day and felt pleasure at being recognized. Several of the faces passing through Summit Terrace were likely famous, too, a fact that astonished him when he thought of how amiable Vernon was with the famous and unheralded alike. To believe the papers was to believe Vernon was a celebrity hound, but Charlie never heard him mention other celebrities and was simultaneously impressed and jealous at how easily commoners like himself were integrated into Vernon's life.

The woman who answered Vernon's door startled him.

"I'm Jessica," she said. "You must be Charlie." Her quick smile indicated that she'd grown used to people like Charlie in Vernon's life. A tattoo of one of the Powerpuff Girls—he didn't know which—peeked over the waist of her jeans as she sprinted for the whistling teakettle. "Would you like some?" Her brunette bob flounced as she reached for a box of tea.

Charlie declined as Vernon burst through the front door, led by a panting white pug on a leash. Vernon dropped the leash and the pug snuffled against Charlie's leg. "I see you've met," he said, indicating Jessica, who was ladling sugar into her teacup. "Oscar, stop."

"We're old lovers, actually," Jessica said.

Charlie demurred, picking up on the vibe between Jessica and Vernon. Instead, he laughed and handed Vernon the envelope with the typed interview. "A first draft," he said.

"Great, thanks," Vernon said. "I'll take it with me." He dropped the envelope on the kitchen counter. "Did you make an extra key for Charlie?" he asked Jessica.

She replaced the teakettle and scowled. "I thought that's what you were doing."

"I was walking the damn dog," Vernon said, exasperated. He unhooked the leash and Oscar bolted for the metal bowl in the kitchen.

"Why didn't you walk him to the locksmith's?" Jessica asked evenly.

Vernon exhaled. "Because I thought you'd already done it."

"I got the mail," Jessica said, her counterpunch landing squarely with Vernon, who dropped the issue of the extra key and took up his mail.

"I'll have to get the key to you another time," Vernon said to Charlie as he opened an envelope from Camden College. For a moment, Charlie worried that the letter was about him. A warning perhaps. The irrational thought passed when Vernon said, "Camden wants my archives." He laughed and flung the letter onto the counter.

"That's an honor, right?" Charlie asked, affecting a false naïveté in case there was something unstated about giving your archives to your alma mater that he didn't apprehend.

Vernon shrugged. "I guess."

"You could get a lot of that junk out of the apartment," Jessica chimed in.

Oscar's bowl skated across the hardwood floor as he dug his face into it, crashing into Jessica's foot. She nonchalantly guided it back to the corner.

"You have to organize it all," Vernon snapped. "You can't just send them a truck full of stuff."

More out of instinct to interrupt the fight than anything else, Charlie said casually, "I can organize stuff if you want."

"An apartment sitter, dog walker, *and* archivist," Jessica said. "Very handy." She smiled playfully at him.

"Oscar is staying with you," Vernon said. "We discussed that."

"We discussed it," Jessica said, "but I didn't agree. I don't want him slobbering all over my place. Plus, my roommate hates dogs."

Vernon sighed.

"It's no problem," Charlie said. His purpose in this scene was apparently to agree to everything. The ease with which he adopted the guise of a sycophant was disturbing to him, but he was powerless to stifle the instinct.

"Do or don't," Vernon said.

"You'll get used to 'do or don't,'" Jessica laughed.

Charlie took the phrase to mean he was fully initiated into Vernon's inner circle, regardless of Jessica's sarcasm.

A buzzer sounded and Vernon picked up the receiver mounted on the wall. "Send him up," he said. "Sorry," he said to Charlie, "can you come by tomorrow and we'll go over everything?"

"I'll bet it's no problem," Jessica mocked, half smiling.

Charlie couldn't discern if the retort was targeted at him or Vernon, and he shrugged it off as Vernon walked him to the door. "Come by early, before I leave," he said. He opened the door and to Charlie's surprise John F. Kennedy Jr. stood in the entranceway, dressed in cargo shorts and a loose green T-shirt, poised to knock. His nearness to JFK Jr. was breathtaking, and an involuntary hitch in his step almost caused him to stumble. He lingered, with a burning desire for acknowledgment and the expectation that Vernon would introduce him. He knew Vernon wouldn't reveal him as the true author of the *George* magazine piece, but a handshake with the famous son of a president would be a treasured memento. He settled for a startled "hello" from JFK Jr.

"See you Friday, then," Vernon said, and waved JFK Jr. into his loft.

Charlie could hear JFK Jr. greet Jessica before the door clicked shut on Oscar's barking. In the perpetual retelling of the encounter, Charlie and JFK Jr. shook hands. Possibly exchanged words. In future tellings, the story would likely be that JFK Jr. complimented him on the ghostwritten piece, and Charlie would come to believe it. With so few witnesses, veracity would be lost in the fog of time.

He punched the button for the lobby and the elevator descended, opening on the second floor. Charlie half expected the woman who smelled so strongly of vanilla to appear, a replication of his previous experience, so it was startling to see the words SMELLY VAGINA spray-painted across the woman's door in blood red. A maintenance guy and an albino in a suit one size too big entered the elevator and spoke in hushed tones.

"How did he get into the building, is my question," the maintenance guy said.

"It's the doorman's responsibility, ultimately," the albino said. "Union will bitch, but this is cause for dismissal."

As the elevator closed, Charlie observed the distinctive V, the same flatness at the fulcrum as in Vernon's signature, which he'd practiced over and over since first seeing it in the inscription Vernon wrote to Olivia.

Jogging down Broadway—he was late for an event that had been on his calendar for at least a month, a reading at the Astor Place Barnes & Noble by Robert Holanda, his creative writing teacher at Glendale Community College—he doubted Vernon had graffitied the door. His brain was still swirling from his late-night escapades, and his synapses clearly weren't firing correctly. Vernon Downs, a famous author, vandalizing his own building. It was too fantastic.

The tiny theater of metal chairs assembled at the top of the escalator on the second floor were mostly unoccupied save for half a dozen people or so. Charlie marveled at the giant poster of the cover of Holanda's new novel, imagining a poster of his own first novel, his name as large as the title. A stench permeated his surroundings and he sourced it to a homeless woman clinging to her tattered plastic bags full of who knew what. He guiltily moved a few rows forward, closer to the podium. From his new vantage point, he could make out the details of the cover image, a blurred Ferris wheel exploding with yellow and red and blue fireworks.

An overweight woman wearing Barnes & Noble green and a lanyard with a badge strolled up to the microphone with a brave face. The loudspeaker annoyed a man in a suit sitting near the front, and he took the book he was flipping through to a quieter corner. As the woman introduced Holanda, mispronouncing his surname, a group of young women paraded in and took seats in the front row, whispering, the distraction compelling the B&N employee to repeat a sentence from her carefully crafted introduction. Charlie recollected two of the women as talentless classmates from Glendale Community College. Their presence in the Astor Place Barnes & Noble was unnerving, and for a breathless moment Charlie wondered if Olivia would be in the crowd, possibly with Shelleyan in tow. The ludicrous was sometimes made possible, as Charlie knew. At the first appearance of Olivia's long, flaxen hair, or the silhouette of her small features, he would retreat into the rows of magazines. He could still hear the transformation in her otherwise sweet voice as she breathed matter-of-factly into the phone, "I just wanted to have a fling with an American," as if answering a question from a stranger. Always able to see all the avenues, he estimated that she had been coerced by her parents. She'd been planning to leave her parents and her homeland behind for good, and somewhere in the house her parents were lurking, listening. He'd nodded solemnly at the click that ended the transatlantic call, adrift in the mystery of what exactly could activate the pulley that would bring her, hand over hand, back to him.

Vernon Downs immediately came to mind. All memories of Olivia not involving her love of Vernon Downs fell away so that when he thought of her, he thought of Vernon Downs, and vice versa.

Holanda appeared from behind a door next to the podium sporting a blue plaid beret, a hat Charlie didn't recollect Holanda wearing at GCC, and smiled at his former students lined up like bowling pins in the front row. Charlie scowled condescendingly at the backs of their heads, their attendance a painful reminder of recent, happier times. Holanda boomed into the microphone as if speaking to a packed hall. Charlie couldn't follow the story, lost in thoughts of how Olivia had been one of Holanda's favorite students, Holanda encouraging her before the rest of the class, which caused some hard feelings among the other aspiring writers, including those currently ensconced up front. It was hard to know if any of them had any real talent—Charlie included—so encouragement had become the foundation of the reward system they all lived by.

After the reading and the short Q&A—and after his classmates had exited the space, tittering about the plans for the rest of their vacation in New York—Charlie approached Holanda, who was signing stock at a table near the podium.

"Charles," Holanda said, standing. "Were you lurking, as usual?"

Charlie smiled and they embraced. "Congratulations on your book. It sounds terrific."

"Can I sign one to you?" Holanda asked.

Charlie knew the hardcover purchase would dent his dwindling credit, but he'd walked into the trap unawares and agreed enthusiastically. The Barnes & Noble employee waited patiently while Holanda scribbled a note on the title page and handed it to Charlie.

"And how is our Olivia?" he asked, returning to the job of signing stock.

Charlie wondered if his desire to attend the reading was actually about this moment. He must've known Holanda would inquire about Olivia, though he'd failed to prepare the pat answer that would rescue him. He hardly suspected himself of a masochistic streak, but as Holanda's question hung between them, he stood mute, his flesh searing. He couldn't answer.

"Oh," Holanda said. "Well, that happens." He continued signing the mountain of books B&N had ordered for the reading, the B&N employee expertly handing over the books open to the title page. "What are you doing in New York?"

Charlie regained his faculties in the face of the question he'd antici-pated. "I'm spending a lot of time with Vernon Downs," he said. "He's become somewhat of a mentor to me."

Holanda arched an eyebrow. The B&N employee fixed on him with sudden interest. "I didn't realize you were a fan of his work."

"I came to it late," Charlie said truthfully.

"I find his stuff to be a little . . . light," Holanda said.

"He's the nicest person in the world," Charlie said. He hadn't antici-pated defending Downs to his former teacher. The opposite, really: He had expected Holanda would be impressed, perhaps asking Charlie to introduce him while he was in town.

"I'm glad to hear it," Holanda said. He finished signing and stood up, stretching. The B&N employee thanked him and carted off the signed books, deserting them in the empty arena. "I didn't want to say this in front of her," Holanda said, nodding toward the retreating bookseller, "but Downs is really a terrible writer. I'm speaking not as a teacher, but as a reader. His books are just gimmicky diatribes contrived to draw attention to himself."

"Have you read his new collection, *The Book of Hurts*?" Charlie asked. He speculated Holanda had only read *The Vegetable King* because of all the press attention—*Minus Numbers* didn't seem like the sort of book readers of Holanda's generation would read—and he'd probably been put out, perhaps even jealous, at all the ink spent excoriating or defending the book.

Holanda shook his head in a manner that indicated he would never, under any circumstances, read *The Book of Hurts*, the answer Charlie had hoped for. "It's some of his more mature stuff," he said definitely.

"I'm glad to hear it," Holanda repeated, and another piece of Charlie's past broke free from his inventory of memories.

Outside, in the dusky triangle of Astor Place, he flipped open the cover of Holanda's book and read the inscription: "To Charlie, who always believed in the possibilities of fiction." He closed the book and carefully placed it on a stack of *Village Voices* inside a plastic kiosk, leaving Holanda's words behind as he trudged toward the subway.

....

Charlie delivered the Obelisk manuscript to the copy editor in Chelsea, as he promised Derwin he would, and decided to walk across town to meet Vernon for the key. The west side of Manhattan had remained a mystery to him, and he gawked like a tourist at the men holding hands in Chelsea, pausing to window-shop for wine he could never afford, loitering out in front of the Hotel Chelsea. He fell into a stream of people flowing down Seventh Avenue, marking Madison Square Garden, people rolling off the escalator under the JumboTron announcing the upcoming Aerosmith concert like products on a conveyer belt. An ambulance roared by and Charlie fantasized about the feeling of rescue afforded the rescued: Someone else in charge of the big decisions, and there's every anticipation that everything is going to turn out okay.

He cut down Thirty-second Street and through the jungle of vendors hawking knockoff designer wear, watches, scarves, and prints of famous landmarks in New York and abroad. Koreatown was a long block of signs in both English and Korean, pictures of deliciously glazed food plastered in restaurant windows. He bobbed down Fifth Avenue, guided by the space oddity of the Flatiron Building. He was perplexed by which direction he should take and guessed incorrectly that either side of the Flatiron would lead him to the East Village. He had to cut across Twentieth Street when Fifth Avenue led him astray, then took Broadway to Union Square, where a farmers' market was in full bloom.

He was still a little early to meet Vernon, so he browsed the stalls, splurging on a hunk of dark chocolate cleaved from a slab the breadth of a manhole cover by a cute girl wearing a yellow bandana. He nibbled the chocolate as he scanned the tables at the Barnes & Noble that loomed over Union Square. Robert Holanda had signed the copies of his book on the front table, and Charlie felt a degree of condescension toward his former teacher. The image of Holanda slinking around town hunting for his own book in bookstores and signing the copies he found, possibly moving them himself to the front table, lowered his opinion of Holanda. He turned Holanda's book over in his hand, smirking at the author photo, reading the blurbs with irony. The writers who had given Holanda blurbs were hardly famous, and he even recognized some as writers who taught at the state universities in Arizona. Holanda could say what he wanted about Vernon Downs, but he'd probably have killed for a blurb from him.

The doorman at Summit Terrace smiled when Charlie approached. "He's not in, but he left this for you." He handed Charlie an envelope with the key, though when Charlie reached the loft, he found the door unlocked. He knocked and then entered. The loft was vacant. All the windows had been thrown open, negating the efforts of the struggling air conditioner. A large television stationed in the middle of the floor played a pornographic movie on mute. "Here boy, here boy," he called out, not remembering the dog's name. No answer. Vernon must've left early and taken the dog to his girlfriend's place against her wishes. He conjectured Vernon triumphed more often than he didn't. He snapped off the television and pushed it back into the corner, closing the windows against the day's heat.

The pull of his unfettered access to Vernon's loft was seductive. He previewed the cupboards, the dearth of any food products or surplus cans of fruit cocktail not a shock, considering how often Vernon dined out. An impressive cache of rum and vodka and whiskey was an unexpected bonus. The kitchen junk drawer was a repository of expired lottery tickets. He slid open the door to the sideboard table and was in awe of the collection of signed books. The books were for the most part unread, but judging by the inscriptions, the authors were either friends or admirers of Vernon's. Charlie hauled out the bins underneath the bed and investigated the trove of work by Vernon, including the prepublication galleys printed by Vernon's publisher in advance of the actual book. Holanda had imparted that galleys were notoriously brimming with mistakes and misspellings, and Charlie casually hunted through the galley of *Scavengers* for typos.

The phone rang, giving him a start. He shoved the bins back under the bed. The answering machine picked up and Vernon's recorded voice boomed sonically. After the beep came "Yo, Vernon, I think I left one of my shoes at your place. Alligator loafer? If not there, then in the cab ride home, dude, so let me know." Charlie rewound the answering machine tape without rummaging for the loafer. He relieved himself in the bathroom, squinting against the white light. As he washed up, he noticed a tube of Aim in the medicine cabinet. He regarded the toothpaste as an archaeological find. *Vernon Downs uses Aim*, he noted. The loft was as intriguing as the lost city of Atlantis, every household article or utensil or effluvium found floating in junk drawers holding an unintended significance. It seemed inconceivable that he once spent an ignorant afternoon hearing about Vernon Downs and *Minus Numbers* from Olivia and Shelleyan, and all these months later he had free reign over Vernon's loft.

The phone rang again, but this time the machine didn't answer. The ringing continued until Charlie realized the source was not the phone, but the intercom system with the doorman.

"Yes?" Charlie breathed into the receiver.

"Someone from *George* magazine is here," the doorman reported.

Charlie wondered if it was JFK Jr. but guessed JFK Jr. would've given his name, or that the doorman would've recognized him.

"Send them up," Charlie commanded, adding, "please."

A few moments later, the elevator arrived and Charlie cracked the door to the loft, as Vernon had done for him the day they met. At the sound of a faint knock, he swung the door open to reveal a young man in his early twenties, his shaved head gleaming in the light. Tiny silver hoop earrings shimmered in both ears.

"I'm here to deliver the proofs for your piece," he said, nervously patting his leather messenger bag.

"Come in," Charlie said, affecting Vernon's cool tone.

"Wow," the messenger said. "Great place."

"Thanks," Charlie said.

The messenger produced a white envelope stamped with the words GEORGE MAGAZINE and CONFIDENTIAL. Charlie spied a copy of *The Vegetable King* in the bag as well.

"Just need you to sign for them," the messenger said meekly. Charlie took the receipt over to the kitchen counter, the nearest writing surface. He began to draw a C on the receipt, when the messenger said, "I was hoping you could sign this, too," and stood apologetically with his copy of *The Vegetable King*. "I'm probably not supposed to ask, so if you don't want to, no problem."

Charlie signed the receipt with Vernon's practiced signature, a perfect counterfeit the result of hours spent tracing the letters in the book Vernon had signed to Olivia. "Be happy to," he said, taking the book. "Who should I sign it to?"

Charlie scrawled the messenger's name onto the title page, his mind humming, the thrill from the deceit producing a kind of mental levitation. He scribbled "Hope you enjoy this" on the title page and repeated Vernon's signature.

"Here you go," Charlie said. "Just don't sell it to the Strand."

"No way, never," the messenger said, bowing slightly. "Thank you." He tucked the novel back into his bag without inspection and did the same with the receipt for the proofs. He thanked Charlie again and drank in the loft. Charlie imagined the stories the messenger would tell his friends back in Brooklyn about his visit to Vernon's.

"I know I missed your Christmas in July party," the messenger said nervously. "But is there any way it would be cool if I came next year? My girlfriend would just die."

"Of course," Charlie said. Granting the messenger's wishes mollified his sense of right and wrong.

"Too cool of you," the messenger responded. He continued to thank Charlie as he called for the elevator, one last thank-you slipping out as Charlie closed the door. He moved in the glow of charity as he opened the envelope to find the proofs of the piece he'd written for *George* magazine. The initial irritation at seeing Vernon's name in the byline subsided as Charlie gaped at his words emblazoned on the page. Vernon hadn't changed so much as a comma. A fantasy quickly developed whereby Olivia would pick up a future copy of *George* magazine based solely on a piece by Vernon Downs in the table of contents, running home to read it, lying across her bed while frantically flipping the pages, his words filling her eyes. He would need to make a photocopy of the proofs as evidence for when he confessed the ruse to her later. The fantasy rewound and replayed through a celebratory tumbler of Vernon's whiskey, continuing through the meal of Chinese takeout he spilled across Vernon's countertop. The scenario, along with the whiskey and Chinese food, lulled him asleep in the early evening.

A clattering woke him near daybreak. He started awake, a blurring figure hovering near the door. The bleary visage of Vernon Downs bore down on him. "Why the fuck are you here?" he asked, his hair tousled as if he'd ridden an all-night roller coaster at Coney Island. Charlie had forgotten to turn off the air-conditioning and the loft was frigid.

"I thought . . . ," Charlie said. "The doorman gave me the . . ."

Vernon jittered through the loft, grabbing up random objects: a fistful of CDs, something from a drawer in the kitchen, the opened bottle of whiskey. "You weren't supposed to come until—," Vernon said. "I mean this is not a good—. Whatever." His eyes were small and red, and Charlie wondered if he was high. "Everything is totally fucked. My fucking dog is missing and I have to leave for Vermont and . . ." Vernon recounted in profane outbursts how Jessica had taken Oscar for a walk and the dog had bolted from his leash. Vernon had canvassed the area around Jessica's Murray Hill apartment before retreating to a Kinkos to produce a flyer he'd spent the early hours affixing to any flat surface he could.

"I'm sorry," Charlie said. "I didn't know."

"You have to be vigilant," Vernon said, a globule of spit landing near Charlie. "If anyone calls about Oscar, you have to go meet them. Here." He dug into his black jeans for his wallet and swiped all the cash, handing it to Charlie. "Just do whatever you have to."

"I will," Charlie promised.

"And call me immediately when you find him," Vernon said.

Charlie nodded and Vernon disappeared into the bathroom among a clattering of toiletries. Charlie quickly counted the money, which amounted to over four hundred dollars. Vernon emerged with a duffel bag and a suitcase on wheels. He'd smoothed water through his hair, and the adrenaline that had fueled his all-night vigil had recessed, leaving him limp, barely able to scrape the luggage across the floor. "I meant to tell you," he said. "The editor at *Shout!* magazine likes your story. He said he'd publish it in the fall fiction issue."

Charlie guiltily longed for Vernon to leave so he could bask in his great fortune. "I can't thank you enough," he said. Vernon waved him off, distractedly checking his answering machine for news of Oscar, deleting the message about the lost loafer before it finished. He trundled into the hall, a rumpled, near lifeless figure, and left without saying good-bye.

III

ON HIS WAY out for coffee, Charlie didn't recognize the new doorman, who was leaner and had a militant air about him. He was also appreciably older than the doorman Charlie'd felt friendly toward. "Where's the other guy?" he asked, but the new doorman just shrugged and returned to sorting some cards on his desk. He reckoned the doorman had taken a sick day, or maybe even a personal day to play hooky. Good for him. Outside, a hulking moving truck idled at the curb. Charlie casually wondered if the woman on the second floor had found another apartment somewhere far away from Summit Terrace.

Waiting at the corner bodega for his coffee and egg sandwich, he flipped through the *Post*, landing on a small item about Vernon offering to name a character after the person who found Oscar. He was amazed at the press's preoccupation with every facet of Vernon's life. Back at Summit Terrace, he exited the elevator to find a woman with a brunette ponytail fidgeting with the lock on her door. "Hold the elevator," she called out, but he had already let the elevator go.

"Sorry," he said as he slid the key into Vernon's door.

"You must be Vernon Downs," the woman said, apparently forgiving the faux pas. "I'm subletting while my sister is in Paris," the woman said, the dimples on her cheeks and the tiny cleft in her chin forming a flawless frame for her soft smile. There was a tomboy element buried deep within, Charlie sensed, a toughness masquerading as delicacy. "I'm a huge fan." She held out a manicured hand. "I'm Christianna."

He returned the smile and shook Christianna's hand. "Nice to meet you," he said. He felt no guiltier about giving this misimpression than he did earlier in the week when someone had mistaken him for someone else, calling and waving from across the street. He'd waved back as a courtesy and the woman moved on. There was little harm in fulfilling expectations, he thought. Besides, he could always plead ignorance with Christianna if the truth emerged, convincing her the miscalculation was her own.

"How long have you lived in the building?" she asked. Uncertain of how long Vernon had been in residence, Charlie was about to cover with "Not long," but Christianna didn't wait for his reply and said, "I just have to say"—she put her hand on his arm—"that the party scene in *Scavengers*, you know, the End of the World party? That's exactly how it was at my college. The tiki torches, everything. God, I'm sorry I missed your Christmas party."

"Oh, really? Where did you go to college?"

"That was at Hampshire. I'm at New Haven now," she said, eager for a reaction. "Drama school. I want to move to New York to be an actress." She called for the elevator and it opened, having never descended to the lobby. "Well, see you around, Vernon," she said, and was gone just like that, the swirl of lilac perfume dying in her wake.

He avoided Christianna over the next week or so, pretending to be in a rush if she waylaid him in the lobby, or in the elevator, or on their adjacent balconies looking down on Thirteenth Street. Christianna's alarming intimacy, as well as her penchant for reciting her favorite scenes from Vernon's works, had become disquieting.

The first time she caught him in the elevator, on his way to meet someone who mistakenly thought he'd located Oscar: "You know what I loved about *The Vegetable King*? The stuff about Huey Lewis and Phil Collins and Whitney Houston. I laughed my ass off when I read it."

The first time she cornered him at the mailboxes in the lobby: "You probably hear this all the time, but that story in *Book of Hurts*, the one set in Hawaii, is one of my favorites."

The time she caught him people-watching on the balcony had spooked him the most. Christianna appeared on her balcony, swaddled in a royal blue cotton bathrobe, and addressed him as one of the characters from *Scavengers*. It was a moment before he realized she, too, was in character. He mimicked deafness and shouted something vague about a phone call he had to make, before scurrying back into the loft, easing the sliding glass door shut.

Two days later, exhausted from following a bogus tip about a dog matching Oscar's description wandering off leash near the World Trade Center, Charlie watched as a silver envelope was thrust under the door, followed by the echo of Christianna's door closing. He opened the elaborately calligraphed invitation to a New Year's in August dinner party and knew he would not be able to devise an excuse grand enough to evade the gathering. The homage to Vernon's party was slightly troubling, a fact that menaced him as he grudgingly dry-cleaned the one suit he owned after discovering that the suits in Vernon's closet wouldn't fit.

In the days before her dinner party, Christianna was noticeably absent from the building, and Charlie happily resumed the task of separating and sequencing Vernon's papers. He rarely left the loft, save for a farewell lunch with Derwin, who was decamping Brooklyn for Fire Island for the rest of August. Derwin was keen for details about the archive project, but in delineating his duties, Charlie admitted that the endeavor was a free-form exercise with little direction, and had been undertaken with more passion on Charlie's part than Vernon's. "My only real responsibilities are to check the mail and to report any important phone messages or e-mail," Charlie confessed. He was too embarrassed to reveal his primary responsibility, finding Vernon's lost dog.

"Your Obelisk training is paying off," Derwin laughed as he picked up the tab for the boozy lunch, the afternoon faded by the time they parted, with plans to reunite back in Brooklyn upon Derwin's return after Labor Day.

Charlie didn't encounter Christianna once, and he began to root for the possibility that the dinner party had been canceled, a hope that was

dashed when a catering van appeared on the afternoon of the appointed
date. He reluctantly dressed, fishing through the leftover liquor for a full
bottle of anything, finding an unopened pinot noir. He paced the loft
until half an hour past the designated time, in order to skip the predinner
cocktails, and then grabbed the bottle and presented himself at Christianna's door.

"Well!" Christianna said dramatically. "This is very exciting!" She was
overdressed in a pale blue gown more suited for a ball, or a fairy tale.
"Welcome," she said by way of introduction to the expectant faces popu-
lating the loft, which had the same floor plan as Vernon's. "You traveled
a long way to be here with us tonight," Christianna added, but the other
guests didn't understand her joke, and he worked the room, shaking hands
with the segment producer at MTV, the budding fashion designer who
lived with her parents in Ronkonkoma, the manager of several rap acts
who kept saying he had to "leave soon," and an actress who turned out to
be Christianna's roommate at Yale. The oldest guest by far was familiar,
and as the bespectacled man offered his hand, Charlie recollected him as
the *Times* reporter from Vernon's Christmas party.

"Peter Kline," the man said. "We met at your party."

"Peter's a reporter for the *Post*," Christianna said helpfully.

Charlie waited for Kline to correct her, but Kline nodded and smiled.
"For my sins," was all he said. Charlie smirked at Kline's having elevated
his journalistic pedigree. *Typical*, he thought as the group gathered around
the hand-carved mahogany table boasting a pewter candelabra in which
cinnamon-scented candles were burning.

The catered meal was served by Christianna, who made no mention
of the food having been prepared by caterers, absorbing compliments like
"This is delicious" and "This is so yummy" as if she'd cooked the food herself, a personality quirk that Charlie found oddly endearing. She exuded
sureness, and he admired how easily she assumed the pose.

Dinner conversation ranged from the vagaries of trying to start a fashion design business to the latest MTV gossip to how hard it was to audition for female directors. Charlie politely solicited information about the rap world from the lone dinner guest who seemed content to sit back and listen, but his questions were answered with a short yes or no and, not really being interested in the subject, he gave up.

Christianna's Yale roommate—she'd been introduced as Diane or Diana, he couldn't remember which, though she'd haughtily corrected the rap manager when he called her by the wrong name—raved about an off-Broadway play she'd just seen having something to do with the Wright brothers and their illegitimate sister.

"I tried out for the part of the sister for the Williamstown festival," Christianna said mournfully.

"You would've slaughtered whoever they have in the lead now," Diane or Diana said.

Christianna smiled appreciatively. "So many parts, so many parts," she said.

"I could never do that," the MTV producer said. "Put myself out there like that. To be judged. I couldn't stand to."

"How do you keep doing it?" Charlie asked, genuinely interested.

"If you keep wanting it, you'll get it," Christianna said simply. "Nobody can take that from you." Christianna and Diane—he'd decided it was Diane—hooked their pinkies in a secret handshake. "Tell us what you're working on now," Christianna said to Charlie.

"Are you a painter?" the fashion designer asked, forking a piece of sweet potato casserole into her mouth.

"You're kidding, right?" Christianna said. "This is one of our greatest living authors. Haven't you read his work?"

"I have," Kline said, raising his hand pointlessly.

The actress turned to Christianna. "Remember that year we watched *Minus Numbers*, like, everyday?"

Christianna nodded.

"Have you seen *Minus Numbers?*" the actress asked, the table turning on the fashion designer.

"Umm, maybe," the fashion designer said.

"That the one with what's-his-name?" the MTV producer asked.

"Oh," Christianna said. "I love him."

Charlie watched this conversation develop with some amusement.

"Julian really needs you right now," Christianna said to the actress, who in turn uttered the next line, the two playing out one of the pivotal scenes in *Minus Numbers* for the benefit of the dinner party. The table erupted in applause and Charlie felt himself bowing in his chair.

Candlelight slowly became the only light, obscuring the guests' faces. Successive bottles of wine were opened, the wine a precursor to cocktails that activated a buzz in his brain. At some point, Christianna left the table to put on some music, the notes of a classical piece fluttering around them like small birds. Between rounds, the fashion designer and the MTV producer and the rap manager begged off. The actress excused herself to go to the bathroom, grabbing the table for support as she rose, and never returned. Christianna would later find her passed out on her bed. Charlie was planning his own exit strategy, the warmth of the food and liquor in his stomach hindering his good-bye, when Kline asked him a question that sobered him.

"How about letting me do a profile," he said.

Charlie pretended not to hear, an absurdity considering the room was empty except for the three of them.

"Who, me?" he asked, hoping to brush off the request.

"You didn't think he meant me, did you?" Christianna asked. She laughed at her own joke, but no one else did.

"What about it?" Kline asked.

"Maybe when the new book comes out," Charlie said.

"When's it coming out?" Kline asked, slipping into his reportorial persona.

"Who knows?" Charlie said. The conversation began to hang heavy around his neck. The candles burned dangerously low, flames skating on pools of wax. He stood abruptly. "Best dinner party ever," he said grandly, bringing Christianna to her feet. "Peter," he said, holding out his hand. "Always a pleasure."

Christianna escorted him to the front door and kissed him on both cheeks only after he promised they'd do it again soon. He made the short walk to Vernon's loft with considerable effort, fumbling the key in the lock. Inside, he threw off his clothes and hopped into the shower to cleanse his mind of the entire evening. He checked Vernon's e-mail, the messages falling into the inbox like snow. He clicked on an incoherent e-mail from Jeremy Cyanin involving a party he'd attended at the Soho Grand. Charlie deduced that Cyanin was speaking in some sort of code he and Vernon shared, which provoked an irrational tizzy about his trying to undermine Charlie's budding friendship with Vernon, and Charlie deleted the e-mail, cleaning out the trash folder as well to erase all traces of it.

An e-mail from a famous writer whose new book was being adapted for film by Tom Cruise asked if he and Vernon were still on for drinks at Lucy's, and Charlie took the opening to inform the famous writer that Vernon had left New York for the foreseeable future, signing his full name, adding "Asst. to Vernon Downs" after reading the e-mail four times for typos. When the famous writer replied that he, too, was in Vermont, as was Lucy's, Charlie switched off the computer to stanch his severe embarrassment; a clutch of days passed before he could bring himself to fire it up again, finding a lone e-mail from a woman named Shannon Hamilton with the subject line "From a fan." He rolled his eyes and clicked on the e-mail.

Dear Mr. Downs,

Where to start? I'm guessing you get a lot of letters like this one, and I'm not sure how much you read before you stop reading, so I'll dispense with the usual chatter about how big a fan I am of your work and go right to the heart of it: Like you, I'm a graduate of Camden College, but unlike you, I'm a writer that no one has heard of. I did my Camden thesis about you and am wondering if you had any advice as I start out into the real world. A lame question, perhaps, but the answer is very important to me, so if you can see your way through to write back, I'd appreciate it.

Sincerely,

Shannon Hamilton

Charlie deleted the message, instinctively discerning that Vernon would not waste his time responding to Shannon Hamilton, but something compelled him to retrieve it. He read the e-mail a second time. Before he realized it, he'd clicked reply and had written, "Dear Shannon." He contended that Vernon wouldn't want to slight a fan over an unanswered e-mail. Better to dispatch with the e-mail, he thought, regarding the chore as one of his clerical duties. He'd mention it to Vernon and they'd both chuckle and then forget about Shannon. Convinced, he touched his fingertips to the keyboard.

Very many thanks for your e-mail. As you might imagine, I get numerous queries such as yours, both through my agent and in my personal mail, but I'm always happy to hear from a fellow Camdenite. (Flattered about your thesis, by the way.) I guess I'd say the best advice is not to let anyone dissuade you from what you want to do. If you want to write, write. Don't take no for an answer. Good luck.

Charlie proofread the e-mail and then typed Vernon's name. A thrill ran through him as he clicked send. He deleted both Shannon's e-mail and his response.

....

Where to start? Charlie thought as he lorded over the boxed archives. A binder dated around the time of the publication of *Minus Numbers* revealed Vernon's previous attempt to chronicle his early years, despite the impression he'd given Jessica when announcing Camden's desire for his papers. He scoured the index to see what had come before, a little surprised by the sentimental entries:

1972.01	Sunshine-gram from Mrs. Ormiston (2nd grade teacher) for excellent penmanship
1973.01	Photo from *Los Angeles Times* dated April 19, 1973, re: Vernon in Cub Scout parade at Rose Bowl
1975.01	Article from Los Angeles newsmagazine dated October 14, 1975, re: Mrs. Cotton's 5th grade class trip to courthouse; incl. photo of VDD
1977.01	Manuscript—"The Mystery of Dead Man's Grave." Original.
1977.02	Pocket Books' declining letter for "The Mystery of Dead Man's Grave," dated April 8, 1977.
1978.01	*No-Name News*—broadside for Fowler Elementary
1981.01	Receipt for private phone line for bedroom
1982.01	Manuscript—"The Last Lemonade Stand on the Block." First draft.
1983.01	Beverly Hills High yearbook—1983

Thoughts of Vernon as a Cub Scout amused Charlie as he read through the index, matching his personal chronology to Vernon's, remembering his own unhappy days against Vernon's popularity at Beverly Hills High, the catalog of manuscripts and love notes faithfully labeled as correspondence; the notebooks and tests for each class carefully maintained, the instructor's name appearing in the binder entry; the letters of recommendation to Camden, Vernon's Camden application, and his acceptance letter the last entries in the archive. Charlie realized that he'd be responsible for cataloging the bulk of Vernon's public life. He eagerly dived into the material. He opened an unmarked box and reached for a black folder containing a sheaf of email from the Bank of America in Sherman Oaks, all sent at the same date and time, the body of the email left blank. He fanned through the printed e-mails, looking for some indication of what they represented—were they documents or correspondence?—and quickly became frustrated by the lack of identifying detail. He was disheartened, too, to find the sealed envelope with the typed interview buried on Vernon's desk, though he had decided to try to publish the interview with a more established outlet than *Oneironaut*, so there was no hurry for Vernon to proof it.

He cracked open a window and let the street noise permeate the loft. The first order of business would be to create piles by year. He marked out a space on the floor for 1982 and then paced off a spot for 1983, and so on. He doubled the volume of the space for *The Vegetable King*, assuming that a preponderance of documents would be dedicated to the controversy the novel had inspired. Next he unpacked the boxes and scattered their contents into their respective spots. In all, it took him two days to separate the material, a feat Charlie celebrated with a tall glass of a leftover cabernet. With the sorting stage complete, he assessed the loft, a paper landscape of letters and reviews and drafts of manuscripts.

After a quick lunch at the Blimpie on the corner, and against the blazing *Minus Numbers* soundtrack, Charlie began picking through the piles. An item he'd previously resisted—a folder marked CAMDEN – ADV. CREATIVE WRITING—called out to him, and he leafed through drafts of early chapters from *Minus Numbers*, line-edited by Vernon's mentor, Harrison McInnis. Charlie hungrily devoured the early work but put the folder away short of the conclusion he was hurtling toward: The early drafts of the novel weren't very good. He agreed with the comments McInnis had written in the margins: "Melodramatic" or "Too dark" or "Is this supposed to be funny?"

A folder from the 1981 pile labeled PHANTASM caught his eye. The folder contained hand-drawn flyers for what apparently was a high school band in which Vernon was the keyboardist. Charlie studied a heavily xeroxed photo of the band posing with the Beverly Hills High auditorium

in the background. A packet of lyrics buried behind the flyers fell to the
floor and Charlie scooped them up, saying the words out loud.

Touch Me   *Words and music by Vernon David Downs*
The touch of your hand
Can tame any man
You're an obsession
No one can have

You walk across the room
And I shiver and shake
My heart's beating faster
I just can't wait . . .

Please!

(Touch me!)
With your tender touch
(Touch me!)
You can't love me too much
(Touch me!)
Touch me all over and you'll see
All I want
Is you to touch me

I don't know what you've got
But I know I want it
I don't know what you've got
But I know it's hot

It's so hard to ignore

Just reach out and touch me
Don't let up
Keep givin' me more

Please!

(Touch me!)
With your tender touch
(Touch me!)
No, no, you can't love me too much
(Touch me!)
T-t-t-touch me
So true
Touch me
I want it all from you
(ad-lib, repeat & fade)

He caught himself singing the lyrics as he pecked his way through the archives, selecting an envelope marked THE ANGEL'S TRIP - CHRISTMAS 1971 that contained a handwritten story about an angel atop a Christmas tree who falls on Christmas Eve and follows the tinsel trail back to the top, encountering villainous ornaments who orchestrated the angel's fall and who prevent her ascent before Christmas morning. Charlie noted the genesis of Vernon's adult handwriting in the child's hand, the disconnected letters, the violent Rs, the pointed Ds. He couldn't imagine the discipline and patience required to stick with a passion from childhood through adulthood. How had Vernon not been diverted by wanting to be a center fielder, or an astronaut, or a lawyer, like practically everyone did? Vernon's tunnel vision gave Charlie hope for his reunion with Olivia. The fact that Vernon had committed to what he loved, and had found success in his fidelity, seemed to bode well for the future, he thought.

The song Charlie liked best on the *Minus Numbers* soundtrack filtered through the speakers, and as he moved to turn up the volume, he skidded on a folder peeking out of the stack for *The Vegetable King*, crashing hard to the floor, causing the CD to skip. He massaged his left knee and could feel the bruise forming under his skin. He kicked at the file folder, trying to shove it back where it belonged. He lifted the stack and pulled the folder free, a swatch of manila sticking to the hardwood floor.

The unmarked folder held a letter from Vernon to someone named Burton LaFarge, dated the previous May.

Hey, Burt,

Your letter shook me up some, especially since I stood up for you when they first talked about kicking you out of Camden. I even went before the administration for you, do you remember that? Hope you do. Hope you remember it as I try to deal with what you're saying re: *The Vegetable King* and the manuscript I helped you with sophomore year. A lot of people sent me stuff that year and I looked at it all, so I find what you're suggesting to be an incredible coincidence. It's been a dark year for me, people coming at me from all directions. Can't use any more bad publicity. Just can't use it. Remember that, Burt? That was your line whenever someone handed you drugs after you were already out of your mind. Just can't use it. I ask you to remember those days as we work through this. Is there any chance you'll come down from the figure you mentioned in your letter? It's a lot of money, as you know. I mean, if that's the figure, then that's the figure. But if there's a different figure, will you let me know?

V-E-R-N-O-N

A business card for a detective agency in Jersey City was paper-clipped to the letter. Charlie replaced the letter and slipped the folder back where he found it, as if he hadn't seen it. He started the *Minus Number*s soundtrack over from the beginning and poured himself a vodka tonic, which stayed the onslaught of questions raised by the letter.

....

Charlie sensed an impending drink invitation from Christianna long before it arrived in the form of spontaneity in the elevator—"I'm meeting some friends at Aviator, would you like to join us?"—and he knew, too, that he would accept, not least because he was addicted to her fawning over him, the Famous Writer. He'd just returned from the Upper East Side, someone having claimed to have found Vernon's dog, but who in reality only wanted to meet Vernon Downs and get him to sign a book, which Charlie obliged. He'd found cataloging Vernon's archives a lonely endeavor, his days taken up with boxes of memorabilia celebrating Vernon Downs's success and with little else, leaving him restless and utterly alone once he stopped shuffling papers for the day. So much so that Charlie began to participate actively in the archives: An envelope containing correspondence with an author Charlie had vaguely heard of sandwiched between drafts of *Minus Numbers* provided the details of a small literary feud involving an article Vernon had written for *USA Today*. Charlie judged the feud to be too trivial to ruin a friendship and penned a short note of apology to the author in Vernon's handwriting.

And so he said yes to drinks at Aviator, though he claimed he needed to meet her there. "Prior obligation," he lied. Christianna was oblivious—did she notice that he hardly left the apartment?—but delighted that he would join her and her friends. In truth, the cash Vernon had left in aid of the fruitless search for Oscar had dwindled, spent mostly on takeout and cabs. Charlie convinced himself that the sustenance and transportation were precisely what Vernon had intended the money for. He further convinced himself that the idea to sell off some of the signed books in Vernon's collection to the Strand to keep liquid—and thereby primed and ready to answer any alleged Oscar sighting—was sound. The first doubts were quashed by Charlie's supposition that authors were always sending Vernon signed books—he'd found three in the mail from debut writers since he began apartment sitting—and so he cherry-picked a dozen or so books and waltzed them over to the Strand, pocketing an easy hundred dollars from the curmudgeonly buyer behind the counter, who raised an eyebrow at the inscriptions but remained silent on the matter. Charlie caught the buyer regarding him, and he signed Vernon's name to the receipt acknowledging the transaction. The buyer gave him a half smile and nodded as he swept the signed books aside and called for the next person in line.

The crowd at Aviator was unusually small, which Charlie ascribed to the hour, just past six. He was two vodka tonics in before Christianna finished her story about an exploitive audition she'd had that morning. "It was a student film," she said. "Guess I shouldn't have been surprised."

"You should turn him in," Charlie said, pulverizing the lime at the bottom of his glass with a red plastic straw.

"I was thinking the exact same thing," Christianna said, sipping her White Russian. "Funny thing was he resembled my friend James. Made me feel a little sorry for him, I guess. He died when he was nineteen."

"Jesus, sorry," he said.

"It's okay," Christianna said, finishing her drink and handing the empty glass to the waiter, who replaced it with a fresh drink. The waiter also set down a plate of mozzarella marinara that Charlie didn't remember anyone ordering.

"How did it happen?"

"He was trying to light a cigarette—well, I'm pretty sure it was a joint, but what does it matter, right?—and his BMW flew off the freeway. I was following him. It was Labor Day weekend and we were going to stay at his parents' place."

"Awful," Charlie said, eyeing the dish between them. He poked at it with a fork, opting to partake in the free food. He presumed that since Christianna had extended the invitation, she would treat.

"He always ordered this," Christianna said with a sigh.

"What," he asked, "White Russians?"

"The mozzarella marinara," she said, sighing again.

He put down his fork, forcing himself to swallow the gooey cheese, trying not to envision it as a chunk of flesh. "Was this when you were at Yale?" he asked.

Christianna bobbed her head, but he couldn't tell if she was indicating yes or no. The story felt familiar and he couldn't figure out why. (Later he would come across a letter in the archives from one of Vernon's friends describing how the story Vernon had written for *The Book of Hurts* about the death of their friend outside Palm Springs—in the exact manner that Christianna had described her friend dying—had helped the friend cope with the loss.) "Speaking of death," Christianna said, launching into a tale about her college roommate OD'ing, which Charlie recognized as being right out of Vernon's novel *Scavengers*.

"So I come back after a night of drinking at the Pub and find her on the floor and it looks like she's not breathing. I look around and see a half-empty bottle of whiskey"—Dewar's in the book—"and think, *Oh my God, she's going to die.* So I grab a freshman in the hall and we drive my room-mate to the emergency room"—Charlie remembered a funny exchange from *Scavengers* about one of the characters thinking the closest hospital was in Keene, New Hampshire, but he stifled his smile at this bit of comic relief absent from Christianna's version—"and the doctor can't find a pulse." Ditto the book. "The doctor says, 'Your friend is dead,' and I'm standing there thinking, *This can't be, this can't be,*" Christianna continued, "and then my roommate opens her eyes and says, 'Am I really dead?' And the doctor says, 'Yes, you are. I can't find a pulse.' Can you believe that?"

He said he could not.

"So I say to the doctor, 'How can she be dead? She's talking!'" Christianna said, shaking her head at the absurdity. "But the doctor insisted. He kept saying, 'Your friend is dead. Your friend is dead.'"

"That is something," Charlie agreed, signaling for another drink. Christianna grew quiet, and he wondered if she'd recounted these plagiarized stories from Vernon's work to test him or to impress him. A game was afoot, but he couldn't grasp the rules. Christianna's left thigh brushed his and he moved away reflexively, wishing he hadn't. A general sexual frustration that had been accruing for weeks begged for an outlet, though he felt sure that sleeping with Christianna would be a monumental mistake. The perceived rebuff chilled the pleasantness the table had enjoyed; if he didn't manufacture an excuse to leave, the two would share a constrained stroll back to Summit Terrace or, worse, he would be made to pick up the check.

"Hey, look," Christianna said, brightening.

Jeremy Cyanin strolled into Aviator in a charcoal suit, leading a dark, petite woman to a table near the bar. "Oh no," Charlie said, slumping down in the booth.

"What?" Christianna asked.

"Great," he said.

"*What?*" Christianna asked again, this time intrigued by his playacting.

He improvised an escape. "Cyanin's been harassing me about some coke he left at my place," he said.

"So?"

"I did it, like, two weeks ago," Charlie said, affecting lament. "And I'm fresh out." He detected a spark in Christianna's eyes at the prospect of participating in the melodrama. "I'm going to try to sneak past him," Charlie said, adding, "the bastard."

"I'll cover you," Christianna said conspiratorially. "I'll go up and talk to him. Distract him."

"No, no," he said. "At all cost, you must not engage him or he'll talk you into drinks, and when he finds out you're my neighbor, he'll weasel his way back to the building and we'll never be rid of him."

Christianna nodded. "Oh, I know the type." She squinted at Cyanin, wrinkling her nose in mock disgust.

"Got an idea," he said, motioning for the waitress, a young girl who didn't look old enough to drink, much less serve. "I want to play a prank on my friend," he said, whispering for no reason. "I want to send a Sex on the Beach to that table"—he pointed to Cyanin's table—"but I want you to say it's from that table." He pointed to a booth in the far corner where two comely lesbians were sitting side by side. "Okay, I'm out of here," he said. He reached for his wallet, but Christianna shook her head.

"I've got this, you've got next time," she said, and before he could process the ramifications of "next time," he had kissed her on the cheek and was slithering along the bar, Cyanin with his back to him, the waitress bending to set the cocktail on his table, motioning toward the oblivious lesbians as Cyanin swiveled in his seat. He could hear Cyanin's explanation to his date: "They're fans, what can you do?" Charlie forged through the crowd, spinning away from a woman at the bar who turned precipitously with a martini in each hand. He grasped for a stool, his balance deserting him entirely, and he could only manage to spring forward, falling helplessly into the crowd pushing its way into Aviator. He collided with Peter Kline, the two of them falling against the hostess station.

"Leaving so soon?" Kline asked.

"I . . . have . . . to . . ." He gestured toward Fourth Avenue.

"I thought we were having drinks with Christianna," Kline said, confused.

He engineered an answer along the lines that Christianna was indeed still inside, but that he was feeling ill and had to cancel. "I'm sorry," he said, and took a step toward Summit Terrace.

"Wait," Kline said. The crowd at the door plunged forward and Charlie found himself alone on the sidewalk with Kline. "I was wondering if you'd like to have lunch," he said.

Charlie nodded, not really concentrating on what Kline was saying.

"Thursday?" Kline asked, hopeful.

"Sure," he answered. He would've agreed to anything short of homicide to abort the conversation.

"Thursday at noon," Kline said. "At Jackson's. The paper is buying."

Charlie nodded idiotically, wanting to object. Someone or something tapped him on the back, but when he spun around, he was bewildered to find no one there, surprised further by the rush of vomit he spewed on the sidewalk, chunks of undigested mozzarella falling like wet clouds tumbling from the sky.

"Hey, you okay?" Kline asked, but he held up his hand and began walking backward, away from Kline and the orange and white stain he'd left in front of Aviator. "See you Thursday," Kline shouted, and Charlie waved his arms wildly, both as confirmation and in protest, but the looming threat of lunch with Kline was less urgent than his roiling stomach, and he felt his way down Thirteenth Street, back to Summit Terrace, spending the night in the tub for its comforting proximity to the toilet.

....

Cyanin's flat voice came at him like an assault. He shrank against the porcelain tub, shivering. Who had let Cyanin into the loft? A thought he hadn't considered spooked him: *Cyanin has a key.* He hoisted himself out of the tub, carefully navigating a splotch of dried vomit that had missed its mark. The loft was quiet again and he peered out the bathroom door, ready to be cornered. But the loft was empty. A cold breeze swirled through the kitchen. A small cyclone of paper danced across the promontory of the highest stack of archives, floating and finally settling at his feet. He quickly shut the window he didn't recollect opening, realizing he was alone.

After a long, revitalizing shower, the blanket shrouding his brain lifted. The flashing light on the answering machine called out to him as he pulled on his jacket, and he pressed the button.

"Hello?" It was Cyanin. "Hello?"

He froze, as if Cyanin were at the door.

"Hello, hello, hello." A pause. "Are you back? You're back. I guess the question is, why? A better question is, what was that shit at Aviator? The best question is, why did I have to read about your return in the *Post*? Call me back." Another pause. "P.S. I slept with those two lesbians."

Charlie erased the message, but it was burned in his memory. He opened the *Post* to Page Six, the notorious gossip column, spotting Vernon's name in bold in the "Sightings" column:

> Bad-boy novelist Vernon Downs was seen stumbling out of Aviator on Fourth Avenue, laughing maniacally at a prank he'd just pulled on his fellow bad-boy novelist Jeremy Cyanin.

He skimmed the column—the notice of the actress arrested for shoplifting (again), this time at an antique shop in the Bowery; the underage pop star caught drinking at a club in Noho; the socialite who fled her suite at the Four Seasons without paying—but he invariably drifted back to the mention of Vernon, dumbstruck at how the *Post* had ascertained this bit of false information. It took half a bottle of Gatorade before he put together that Kline was most likely the author of the gossip. Infuriated, he pounded on Christianna's door, the brass knocker vibrating under his fist. He heard Vernon's answering machine through the open loft door: "Vernon, it's Daar. Are you back? Why are you back? Call me." He erased the message, wondering if the *Post* article would reach Vernon. He remembered Vernon's description of his self-imposed exile in Vermont—"submarine down" were his exact words—and hoped that there weren't copies of the *Post* onboard that submarine. He couldn't imagine Vernon caring about the gossip item upon his return at summer's end and found solace in this rationale, which he also applied to the e-mail response from Shannon Hamilton:

Dear Mr. Downs,

Thanks for replying. I appreciate your taking the time. And I'll take your advice to heart. Really. So thanks. I meant to ask in my last e-mail: What was it like when your first novel was published when you were so young?

Your fan,
Shannon

Charlie smiled. He was still grinning as he grabbed a six-pack of Corona from the reach-in cooler at the deli on the corner with one hand and a couple of limes from a plastic basket on the counter with the other, opting for a little hair of the dog over the bagel sandwich he'd set out for. Back in the loft, he opened a Corona and shoved a wedge of lime down its neck, taking a long pull as the computer warmed up again. He unearthed the typed interview, spreading the pages out before him. He opened Shannon's e-mail and clicked reply.

Dear Shannon,

Seems strange to me to be thinking about that book again after all these years. The last time I reread it, I remember thinking I was too young to write a book like that. I also remember thinking that I shouldn't have taken a lot of the editorial advice I received. The first draft of *Minus Numbers* was very, very long and a lot of melodramatic things happened. But what I was going after was to have all these melodramatic things drifting in and out of the characters' lives and to have the power of these melodramatic things completely diminished because of all the fluff that's surrounding their lives. So there could be murders and rapes, but all this other garbage floating around the characters mutes the power of these horrifying things happening to people. This idea probably interested me the most when I was working on *Minus Numbers*.

When the book was edited down—and it was pared down a lot—by the
editing process, a thirty-or-so-page sequence near the end of the book was
left intact and stands out as way too melodramatic. I think the book holds
up until then, but then I just find it to be a little embarrassing. Everything
pretty much reads as I wrote it, but since a lot of stuff was edited out of the
middle, these last pages really bother me, or did bother me when I last reread
it. I also think the editing toward this kind of ending probably helped make
Minus Numbers a more popular book too, and it helped make it a more successful book than it perhaps would've been if I'd had my way.

Yours,
V-E-R-N-O-N

Dear Mr. Downs,

Wow, thanks for that insider's look into the publication of *Minus Numbers*.
Sounds like publishers really have the ultimate say, huh? Sucks. Curious
about your writing habits. And about your favorite books. But if you don't
have time to write me back, don't worry. I've taken up too much of your time
already!

sh

The seduction of the lowercase signature was a whisper that hovered,
filling the room with promises and praise: *Shh, this is between us. Shh, I'm
your biggest fan. Shh, trust me with all your secrets.* He shuffled the pages of
the interview and stroked the keyboard:

Dear Shannon,

I don't write every day. I think about writing every day, but I don't write
every day. There are days where I write a lot, and there are days where I can't
do it. Some days I have either notes or parts of things that I put into my
computer, reorganize, or edit. It really depends on what's going on in my
life, it really depends what kind of mood I'm in. Sometimes the material

overrides the mood and makes you push forward and say, "I really want to do this, I have the impulse to do this right now, I'm gonna do it." And there are other days where you feel like crap and you can't do it. You can't will a good paragraph, you can't wish it to work out. You've really got to be in a mood, and there are a lot of times where I just sort of wander around the apartment, wait for the mail, open up the refrigerator, wait for the mail some more, open up the refrigerator, turn on MTV, hope I get some good magazines in the mail, walk around the corner, go to a movie, things like that.

As for books, my advice is to read whatever you can get your hands on.

V-E-R-N-O-N

Charlie crawled into bed. He couldn't shake the fantasy about how he'd respond if a fan note from Olivia appeared in Vernon's inbox. The idea electrified him no end.

....

Charlie flipped back and forth through the weathered copy of *Zagat* he found in Vernon's top desk drawer, but Jackson's was not listed. Knowing that restaurants in New York sometimes had their official name and their popular name, he searched the index for the name of the restaurant Kline had suggested. Charlie was running late anyway—a burst of energy had propelled him through a midnight session with the archives; he was through 1993 now—but he'd use his inability to locate Jackson's in *Zagat* as his excuse, rubbing it in Kline's face as a salve for what little irritation remained from the Kline-inspired *Post* article. He finally called information, the operator informing him that Jackson's was on West Fifty-fourth Street, and the cabdriver circled the block before finding the unmarked place with blackened windows. Charlie stuck his head through the front door, his eyes adjusting to the dim light made dimmer by the crushed-velvet walls and ceiling. He spotted Kline waving wildly from a table next to the kitchen.

"You made it," Kline said benignly.

"Place is hard to find," Charlie said, his rising annoyance competing with the kitchen clatter. *Vernon wouldn't sit by the kitchen*, Charlie thought.

"This is an old newsman's hangout," Kline said proudly, as if he'd invited Charlie to his private club.

"It's a little dingy," Charlie said. He hoped Kline wouldn't recognize that he was wearing the same suit he'd worn at Christianna's dinner party, then realized he didn't really care. The criticism about the restaurant stung Kline, and Charlie let go of any residual anger about the *Post* gossip piece.

"The food's good," Kline offered.

Charlie had readied himself in case Christianna had told Kline about how he'd taken her to the apartment of the famous actor who lived on Central Park West, an invitation extended by e-mail from Vernon's film agent, someone named Bill Block. "He really wants to meet you," Block had written. Charlie was a fan of the actor, as was Christianna, and they'd spent an animated evening in the actor's company, drinking expensive bourbon from cut crystal glasses while overlooking Central Park. Charlie signed some first editions of *Minus Numbers* and *The Vegetable King* before they left, the actor calling him "mate" as they waited for the private elevator. But Kline seemed oblivious of this latest escapade, and Charlie endured his soliloquy about how he had become a reporter, how he'd come to work for the *Post*, how he coveted a job covering the Yankees. Charlie focused instead on his steak tartare, zoning out on Kline, trying to remember when he'd last eaten steak tartare, if ever. He intended to soak Kline for the best lunch possible.

"So, that was something about what happened when *The Vegetable King* came out, eh?" Kline asked, slipping the question in at the end of a long dissertation about power hitters in the American League. "Seems like it came out of nowhere."

Charlie nodded. "It *was* sudden," he said. "But if I look back over it, there were a lot of warning signs. The publisher not publishing the book was the most sudden thing, though. All that stuff about the cover designer and the in-house personnel complaining about the content of

The Vegetable King was really just background noise until the publisher dropped the book."

Kline held his water glass in midair. "Who told you the book was cancelled?"

Charlie relished the attention and paused dramatically before answering. "My agent called and said, 'Listen, we're going to have to move this book because they're not going to publish it,'" Charlie said. "I was *floored*. It really, really shocked me. And when the editor called to say that this was in fact the case, I was numb. I guess I thought they would publish it, and people would be upset by it, but I would've never guessed with a million guesses that they wouldn't publish it. It was genuinely shocking."

"Dessert, gentlemen?"

Kline waved off the waiter before Charlie could pad the bill with a custard he'd spied on the menu.

"Where did you get the idea for *The Vegetable King*?" Kline asked. "If that isn't too banal a question."

Charlie sighed. "If I had a dollar."

Kline feigned an apologetic look but waited for the answer.

"Let's see," Charlie said, staring into the space of the near-empty restaurant. He tried to recall Vernon's words, thrilled with Kline's rapt attention. "I knew I wanted to write a book about New York—I find the city inspiring—and when I moved here after Camden, I found myself in the midst of all these guys who worked on Wall Street—brothers and friends of my friends from Camden—and I thought, *Perfect, this is perfect*. These guys were making a tremendous amount of money—hollow money, really—for doing next to nothing, which was a metaphor I liked."

"So you were hanging out with them?" Kline asked.

Charlie shot him a look. "Yeah, that's what I said."

Kline waited for the rest and Charlie made him wait for it. He waved to the waiter. "I'll have the custard," he said. "You want anything?" he asked Kline.

"Coffee," Kline said.

Charlie waited for the waiter to bring the custard and the coffee before restarting his story, as a penalty. He was having great fun and he appreciated why Christianna engaged in such role-playing.

"You were saying," Kline said, stirring cream into his coffee.

"Yeah, so I was hanging out with these yuppies," Charlie continued, "after they'd get off work. We'd meet at Harry's, usually, and I'd just sit and listen while they raved about their summer place in the Hamptons, or their new model girlfriend, or some great car they were thinking about buying. It was wild. And so I knew that was the tipping point to start writing the novel. Also"—Charlie stopped for a bite of custard—"the book is informed by a severe black period I was experiencing then, which is why I often refer to it as the most autobiographical of my books."

"It's really an incredible book," Kline said. "Do you ever wonder how it would've fared if it hadn't had all the prepublication hoopla?"

Charlie shrugged. "Guess we'll never know." This wasn't the answer Kline was looking for, which pleased Charlie. "Hey, this custard is first-rate. Think I'll have another." He registered his order with the waiter, who brought another bowl.

"It must've been pretty traumatic," Kline sympathized.

"In some ways it damaged my reputation, probably," Charlie said through a mouthful of custard, "but in other ways it completely enhanced it. See?" Kline nodded as if he understood. "I guess it made me wary of the publishing business—editors always covering their asses, et cetera, but I don't really see the experience as anything but positive. In the end I got to publish the book I wanted to publish, and people got to read it, end of story. I doubt the experience left any sort of imprint on my life, though."

"You're a stronger man than I am," Kline laughed. "I would've held a grudge against all those who tried to ruin the book. At the very least, I would've been angry at the boycott organized by NOW."

"I was angry at the time," Charlie said. "But their puppet show was revealed when they called for a boycott of not just the book, but the products and services mentioned in the book. American Express must've been laughing their ass off about that."

Kline emptied his coffee cup. Two men wearing harried expressions entered, and one saluted Kline, who saluted back. "Colleagues," he explained, though Charlie hadn't asked.

"Last question," Kline said. "What do you think people get wrong about you?"

Charlie laughed and reclined in his chair. "I think everything that's been said about me is pretty much dead on. Or I should say, I don't think there's been anything said about me that I strenuously disagree with," he said. "Sometimes I read profiles of myself written by newspapermen I don't know"—Charlie paused for effect—"and I don't recognize the person they're describing. It's usually just a convenient version of me, but it isn't who I really am. What might not be true is that people assume I wrote *The Vegetable King* for reasons other than the simple fact that this was a book that I needed to write. That would be untrue. But other than that . . . people just write what they want to write." An urgent need broke Charlie's concentration. "Where's the head in this joint?"

Kline indicated the men's room and Charlie slid out of his chair. "If the waiter comes, order me a coffee." He strolled down the hallway to the bathroom, passing a waiter whose face he could barely see in the darkness. He laughed at how Kline had fallen for the charade and slipped out the back, silently bidding Kline adieu.

The new doorman at Summit Terrace, whose name Charlie still hadn't learned, regarded him as he blew through the lobby, hurrying to sign some of the copies of Vernon's work in order to catch the book buyer at the Strand before he left for the day.

....

Unlike the calls from Staten Island, Harlem, and even Westchester County, the sighting of Oscar on the Lower East Side seemed plausible. But the twins in the Grand Street loft were another imposture. They beseeched Charlie to take their manuscript, a novel involving talking cats, and he grabbed the pages and deposited them into the first wire trash bin he encountered. Responding to phantom dog sightings was his most important responsibility, he knew, but he grew to dread them. Charlie no longer cared about the dog's fate. Oscar likely had a new owner and was being fed and petted by the next set of hands, which was just the way it turned out sometimes.

He was startled to find Jessica in the loft.

"I didn't mean to frighten you," she said calmly as she crouched, a green agate pendant swinging on the end of a necklace made of tiny purple beads, sorting through the selection of DVDs stored under the television. Dark circles ringed her eyes. Charlie hadn't noticed the storage space, and the discovery piqued his curiosity about what else might be hidden in the loft. "I see you've made yourself at home." She nodded toward the assemblage of takeout containers and empty beer bottles forming a small cityscape on the kitchen counter. Mountains of paper littered the loft. Charlie hadn't even had the chance to utter "Hello," and he guessed that Jessica was adept at controlling conversations. "I suddenly *had* to see this movie," she said. She plunged her hands deep beneath the television, mining an assortment of foreign films and pornography that didn't seem to embarrass her. "You haven't seen it, right?"

"Which?"

"The one where the guy is trying to get back to his apartment and he's out of money and can't. His money floats out the cab window. He tries to take the subway, but they've raised the fare and he doesn't have enough."

The movie sounded familiar, though he couldn't name it. "Something with mannequins," he offered.

Jessica snapped her fingers. "Yes, exactly. You know it."

"I don't *know* it," he answered. "I may have seen it."

"What's it called?" she asked hopefully.

The phone shrieked and they both froze, waiting for the answering machine. Vernon's voice floated through the loft, swarming around them in deep tones, and Jessica hugged herself absently. Charlie peered into middle space in an effort to coax the title of the film, counting the seconds left in the answering machine message he now knew by heart. The caller hung up without leaving a message and Charlie shrugged.

"I thought you were supposed to be useful," Jessica teased as she returned the DVDs to their rightful place. Charlie admired the seam of Jessica's blouse, tracing it along the curves as it rose and dived this way and that. She stood and Charlie looked absently out the window, causing her to glance over her shoulder.

"I'm told I'm very useful," he said. In his mind, the retort was flat and uninflected, a cold piece of steel brandished as a weapon against any misunderstanding that might arise between them, her being Vernon's girlfriend. Later, after Jessica had left empty-handed, he blamed the disconnect between his intention and his playful tone for the exchange that followed.

"I'll bet." She smiled, closing the distance between them. He smelled a lemony soap, her freckled skin close enough to touch. "What did Vernon tell you about me?"

Her expectant gaze knifed him with guilt. Vernon hadn't so much as uttered a word about her. Charlie didn't even know her last name. He became flushed with the same rank embarrassment he'd felt earlier, at a Starbucks upon his return from the false lead on the Lower East Side. Two overweight girls, both with hair dyed unnatural colors, obviously in high school—and obviously in glee club by the way their conversation was punctuated with outbursts of song—earnestly promised to marry each other if they weren't married by their late twenties. "Do you promise you'll marry me?" the one asked. "Absolutely," the other agreed, "except for the physical stuff, obviously."

Jessica read his reaction accurately. "Not surprised," she said. A shadow crossed her face as she bit her lip. "It's hard, Charlie. Very hard to be with someone who doesn't see you exclusively."

Charlie inadvertently raised his eyebrows.

"He didn't even tell me where he was going," she said, her voice infused with a soft whine.

"You mean where in Vermont?" he asked.

She looked at him askance. "He didn't even say he was going to Vermont," she said bitterly. "Let me guess, Richard is with him, right?"

"Who is Richard?" Charlie was desperate to exit this line of inquiry and hoped to devise a change of topic while Jessica ranted about Richard.

"He's a protégé, like you," she spit out. "A fucking waiter at the Gramercy Park Hotel. Classic. Just classic. The never-ending train of wannabes is tiring. 'Do or don't' extends to his sex life, too, and it's mostly 'Do.'"

The shocking reality of Vernon's bisexuality—Charlie was terrible at guessing people's ages, so naming their sexuality was outside his abilities if asked—was overshadowed by the realization that Vernon and Richard the waiter from the Gramercy Park Hotel had absconded to Vermont, leaving Charlie to dicker with dog sightings and jealous girlfriends. An aberrant hurt at Vernon's not coming on to him passed. Perhaps it meant Vernon took him seriously as a writer. Once the shock receded, he resisted the bitter feelingthat even though he was orbiting Vernon's world, he was a faraway, unnamed planet.

"I guess I need to find my own protégé, eh?" Jessica asked.

Possession overtook him as he regarded Jessica. Had she really come over to look for a DVD? The scheme seemed impossibly juvenile. If you encounter an embittered girlfriend crouched in your space, if only temporarily your space, what are the gears in the machinery that brought her to you? And if you're both feeling betrayed and looking for consolation, what is allowed and what is forbidden? He could reach out. He could touch her on the arm, signaling his submission to whatever purpose she'd arrived at, riven with the idea that she could deliver him from his subordination. Every apprentice was one part assassin.

"I could ask around," Charlie offered, floating it as a joke to gauge Jessica's reaction. The suggestion caught and she narrowed her eyes. She crossed her arms and her smooth biceps flexed involuntarily. He wanted to break the long gaze between them but knew that to do so would be to lose the powerful cord they were momentarily tethered to.

"I'd need someone discreet," she continued. She moved toward the stereo. An old copy of *Details* magazine featuring a profile Vernon had written about the actor Val Kilmer caught her attention and she turned the pages absentmindedly.

"I thought you weren't exclusive," Charlie said, leaning against the kitchen counter.

"I'd like to be," she admitted, the confession squandering a measure of the playful tension that had been building. "I'm normally a one-man kind of girl." She tossed the magazine back toward the pile of media he'd carefully gleaned from the rest of the archives, fluttering the mountains of correspondence, fan letters, and manuscript drafts.

The moment for conquest—if it really existed—slipped away with Jessica's acknowledgment of her true desires. The erotic haze that had briefly hung over them cleared, leaving him stifled and slightly sick to his stomach.

"But if, when you're out serving your master, calling 'Here boy, here boy' around the neighborhood, you run into a suitable candidate, give me a shout," she said, swinging her pocketbook over her silky shoulder. "Don't look too hard, though," she added. "For the dog, I mean." She glided for the door.

"Why not?" he asked, turning but not following.

"Sucks to have something you love withheld," she said.

Charlie took a step toward her. "You took the dog?" he asked.

"He only cares about the dog because it's new," she said. "I was new once too. So were you. Remember that."

"Will you bring him back?" Charlie asked. "We'll say that he just came home on his own. Vernon will never have to know."

Jessica opened the door and grimaced. "What makes you think I still have it?" she asked, and then was gone.

....

"Hurry the hell up," Christianna called from the other side of the screen. She hunted through a Depeche Mode CD, sampling the first beats of each song before skipping ahead.

Charlie reread Shannon's e-mail:

Did you write a draft of the screenplay for *Minus Numbers*? Were you involved with that process? If you had to rank your books according to how successfully you completed what you started out to do, how would that list go?

The titillation of writing Shannon while Christianna waited in the loft was palpable.

S,

I was still in college when I found out they were going to turn it into a movie. I was sent a script by someone, I saw a couple of more scripts, but I was not involved in the process. I didn't want to be involved. When I was first asked if I wanted to be involved, I realistically didn't think I could do it because I was finishing up school, and then I did go back a week later to my agent and said, "Well, maybe I do want to do this." She said, "It's too late, I already told them you don't, and you should finish school anyway." But you know what? I would've done the first draft and it would've been very close to the book and there's no way they would've made it. This was a movie that should never have been made by a big studio, and it should never have been a big, glossy Hollywood movie filled with a lot of stars, directed by a very slick video director. It just shouldn't have been done. It probably would have been much more successful if it had stayed true to the book and was made on a very low budget. There was no way that a big Hollywood studio run by the parents of the children in the book were going to make an honest movie out of that book. So it was hopeless anyway. I could've written a draft, but it wouldn't have mattered.

As for ranking, wow. You have an idea for a book and you're really lucky if you get fifty or sixty percent of that idea down. In your head, you have this grandiose idea of a great, awesome book where you're going to write about this, or this, or this, and when you start writing, reality sets in and you kind of get to the point where you think, *Okay, if I can just get through this, if I can just move it on to here, I'll have done some work and it will have worked out.* Sometimes writing a novel can be so overwhelming and so exhausting emotionally that you're really lucky if you can get fifty or sixty percent of what you really wanted to initially down on paper. I think, for example, *The Book of Hurts* is probably sentence for sentence the best writing I've done by far. I don't know if it's the best book, but I do think that the writing is, let's just say, very unembarrassing to me. I still think *Scavengers* is the one book that I really got down everything that I wanted to do. I wrote a book that really threatened to annoy a great many people. At the same time, I just really have a soft spot in my heart for *Scavengers*. That might be because *Minus Numbers* and *The Vegetable King* were these big bullies that could take care of themselves. *Scavengers* was so slammed because it was about these really annoying, atrocious kids nattering on and on about their lives at college and "Oh, he doesn't love me" or "She doesn't love me" or whatever. It got a tremendous amount of flak that I thought really wasn't due the book. So I sort of have a soft spot for it.

I really can't reread the books, it doesn't really interest me that much. They define a certain time of my life and what was going on during that time of my life, and I don't know, to me they're not that interesting to reread again. They were interesting to write, but to reread them . . . I don't know if I'd get that much pleasure out of that. Or if it would be particularly instructive.

Charlie proofed the e-mail against the typed interview and sent it. He checked Vernon's inbox for anything that seemed urgent. A request from his paperback publisher was difficult to decipher and he decided it could wait. Practically everything could wait, he guessed. At first, he expected daily phone calls demanding updates on Oscar; but the silence from Vermont portended that nothing that was going on in New York was of any importance to Vernon. He heard Christianna open the refrigerator and exhale a long "ew."

"It's nine-*thirty*," she whined. "I thought we were having drinks at Aviator."

Didn't we do that already? he thought. He moved to switch the computer off just as a reply from Shannon drifted into the inbox. His intuition that an unhappy Christianna was a dangerous Christianna warned him that he should save the e-mail for later, but Shannon on the other end of the connection, hoping to catch him in real time, was irresistible.

It seems like it would be easier to write "nice books." It seems you risk so much with technique, with the things you do. At a certain point don't you think, is it worth it?

So much risk, so much risk. He flipped through the typed interview to find Vernon's answer to a similar question Charlie had asked previously, dispirited by the apparent unoriginality of his interview questions. How many times had Vernon had to answer the same question, or some version of it?

It's very strange to me that you say this because in the end it's really not a choice. It's really just a reflection of the writer, whether the subject is vampires, Japanese businessman taking over Los Angeles, evil corrupt law firms, or whatever. It's just a reflection of who you are. I don't think you can force yourself, at least not to the end of an honest book, to write in a way that you don't really want to write. You write how you write. Some people will like it, some people will not like it. But it's not really about pleasing people or making people understand things. Writing is really a very selfish thing. You're writing a book because *you* want to write a book and *you're* interested in these characters and *you're* interested in this story and *you're* interested in this style and *you're* basically masturbating at your desk with all these papers and these pens, and if it goes out there, hits a nerve, fine; if it doesn't, well, fine too. It's really about expressing yourself in a lot of ways, *to* yourself and not to anyone else. You're pleasing yourself when you're writing, you're not pleasing a bunch of other people. You're not constructing a little candy house, or a little gingerbread house that everyone can take a piece of and feel sweet and nice and that makes themselves feel good about themselves or about reading a book. Writing a book is actually a very selfish and very aggressive thing. You're writing this book and putting it out there and it says, *Read me! Read me! Read me!*

He sent the e-mail. His stomach rumbled just as Christianna's patience reached its limit. "Let's go," she demanded.

They negotiated the crowd at Aviator, his brow sweaty from the short walk through the humid August streets, as Christianna steered them toward the same table, creating a sense of déjà vu.

"You should never keep a lady waiting," Christianna chided him. "Tsk, tsk."

"A lady never complains," he joked.

"Oh, you are such a beasty," she said.

"How's that?" he asked.

"You are such a total beasty."

Charlie remembered this bit of dialogue from a Christmas party scene in *Minus Numbers*—it was possibly the only line from the book to appear in the movie—and he scoured his memory for the next line. He concentrated through four swallows of his vodka tonic before Christianna uttered, "You're such a Grinch," a line from a Christmas party scene in *The Vegetable King*, confusing him, though he knew the next line from that scene.

"Bah humbug," he said.

Christianna delivered the response without missing a beat. "What does Mr. Grinch want for Christmas? Has he been a good boy?"

The scene between Nick Banks and his girlfriend, Evelyn, came back to him with clarity—it had been one of Olivia's favorite scenes—and he fell into his role effortlessly, trying to remember his lines. "I want a Gucci wallet, I want a silver sherbet scoop from Lotus, I want a car stereo—"

"But you don't *even* have a car," she said, as if on cue.

"But I *need* a car stereo," he said.

"We'll see what we can do," she said.

Eventually Christianna would respond only to "Evelyn," and Charlie asked twice if she wanted to leave once Aviator was overrun with the preclub crowd. Christianna didn't answer, but Evelyn finally said, "Let's go to the Soho Grand," and he instructed the cabdriver to the corner of Canal and West Broadway. After a couple of rounds of fifteen-dollar margaritas, paid for with the last of his Strand money and served to them while they lounged on oversized armchairs in the hotel air-conditioning, Christianna-as-Evelyn wanted to get a room, a fact she communicated by sitting on his lap and whispering it in his ear, and even though he didn't remember this particular scene from the book, he obliged, the girl at the front desk saying "Welcome back" when he charged the room to his American Express card. The confluence of alcohol and the possibility of sex was amplified when he spied Jessica at the bank of elevators dressed in a black miniskirt and halter top, hanging on Jeremy Cyanin's arm. Her gaze penetrated the dim lobby and she smiled as the elevator claimed them.

When he woke back in the loft, an empty bottle of vodka resting on its side next to the bed, Christianna in her loft, blaring the soundtrack from *Flashdance*, Charlie replayed his memories of the previous night, substituting Jessica for Christianna until the reverie seemed authentic.

Charlie drained a glass of orange juice, toeing the unmarked folder containing Burton LaFarge's letter as he shuffled to the kitchen for a refill. A faint knock gave him a start. He knew who it was and refilled his glass quietly, gliding noiselessly back to the computer.

An e-mail from Shannon erased any further thoughts about Christianna.

What did you want to be before you wanted to be a writer?

The lone question bespoke a familiarity that was both alarming and alluring. Gone were the days of "Dear Vernon," and Charlie lamented the disappearance of Shannon's lovely electronic signature, the tiny *s* and *h* importing its own message. He hoped to revive the tradition by not falling victim to the new parlance, instead addressing Shannon as always.

Dear Shannon,

  Before I was a writer I wanted to be a musician. In fact, I still have fantasies of being a musician, and that's one thing I definitely was going to embark on before Camden. I was in a band in high school—Phantasm, which was not the name I thought of, but one the guitarist did. It was the summer before going to college. I had been accepted to Camden, and it was that summer where the decision was either to stay with the band and see what would happen, or go to Camden and major in creative writing, read everything, and start to concentrate on that. Being the really kind of wimpy, safe adolescent I was, I choose to go to college, and the band broke up.

V-E-R-N-O-N

The orange juice was impotent against the hunger seizing him. He dressed haphazardly and listened at the door before exiting by the back stairs. Breakfast at Baxter's, the diner on First Avenue, was the remedy. The diner had started to feel more like a sanctuary than the loft on Thirteenth Street, so he was dismayed to look up from his omelet to find a college-aged kid with dirty-blond dreadlocks standing beside his table.

"Mr. Downs?"

"Yes?"

"I'm Shannon," the young man said, flipping his sunglasses up on his head. A day-old beard camouflaged a ridge of adolescent acne scars on Shannon's wide chin.

"Oh," he said. "Hello."

Charlie bit down on the inside of his cheeks to squelch both his supreme disappointment and the anxiety of having been watched. Though he never imagined meeting the recipient of his late-night e-mail correspondence, he'd nonetheless begun to fantasize about what Shannon might look like, mostly a compilation of the best features of girls he'd known. Olivia had been curiously excluded from the anthology, which he attributed to the illicit thrill of cheating on his own feelings whenever he answered one of Shannon's e-mails. All that mental expenditure was gone, but the need to delicately extricate himself overtook his anger at what was clearly an inappropriate situation.

Shannon towered nervously over the table, fingering the strap on a new messenger bag. Charlie masked his annoyance by asking Shannon to sit.

"Thanks," Shannon said.

"How did you know who I was?" Charlie asked. "I mean, how did you recognize me?"

"I saw you come out of the building," Shannon answered, momentarily embarrassed.

"How did you know where I lived?" Charlie asked.

"Oh, um, hope it's okay," Shannon said. "The alumni office at Camden gave me your address when I asked for your e-mail."

"Oh," Charlie said. The pain of recognition was unbearable. "So. You're a . . . man."

He'd hoped for levity as a stall tactic, but Shannon blushed. "Um, yeah. Did you think—"

Charlie cut him off before the embarrassing realization could land. "Just an observation," he said.

"I wanted to, um, thank you for, you know, taking the time to write to me," Shannon said, the mangled sentence barely making its way from his lips. "I'm, uh, sure that you have better things to do."

"No problem," Charlie said, regaining his composure. He was the famous writer, after all. "Happy to help."

"It's really nice of you," Shannon said.

Charlie sipped his coffee. "You live in the East Village?" he asked.

"Hoboken," Shannon said.

The two sat in silence and Shannon's nerves gave first. "I, uh, was hoping you would read my book," he said, hoisting a manuscript from his bag. "And, you know, you wouldn't have to line-edit it or anything. Unless you wanted to."

Charlie sipped his coffee again, stalling.

"Fine," he said.

Shannon stood, gazing at his watch. "Anyway, I hope it's not a bother and thanks again. Take your time. I gotta run. Nice to meet you."

"Likewise," Charlie said. He ordered another cup of coffee, relieved, his dull headache receding with every slurp. He fanned the pages of Shannon's manuscript, embarrassed at the revelation that Shannon was not a sexy female fan, but was instead just another male writer who wished he were Vernon Downs.

....

Shannon dropped an e-mail a week later crafted to seem innocuous—"Have you had a chance to read my manuscript yet?"—and Charlie answered quickly that he had, and that he liked it. He hoped this was all the encouragement Shannon sought, but Shannon persisted to know what exactly he had liked, and he generalized about the originality of the main character's plight as well as the role chance played in the lives of all the characters. Shannon assailed him with direct questions about the manuscript, but his deft circumlocution kept Shannon at bay until, weary, Shannon asked him point-blank if he would recommend him to his agent. The query came after a long day of e-mailing wherein Charlie tried to make up for his brutal evasiveness by actually reading the first chapter of Shannon's manuscript—he discovered he'd been spelling the main character's name wrong, which likely as not had aroused Shannon's suspicions—and so he answered, "Yes, I will." Shannon replied with a smiley face drawn with a colon and a closing parenthesis.

Another e-mail the next day was devoid of any pretense of endearment. Shannon asked again if Charlie would recommend him to Daar Baumann and again Charlie promised that he would. Shannon thanked him, adding, "I was thinking it might be helpful to have a blurb from you. Possible? Thanks. Your fan, Shannon."

"Hey, Shannon"—Charlie hoped the casual salutation would temper Shannon's aggressiveness—

> You should send the whole manuscript. She'll want to read it front to back, guaranteed. Give her this quote from me:
> "With this novel, Shannon Hamilton pulls off a magic act of sustained imagination. Hamilton's prose sings, his characters intrigue, and I have no doubt the publication of this book will bring favorable comparisons to some of our most revered authors, not least among them Salinger. This book is an updated *Catcher in the Rye*."

Charlie appended the note with Daar Baumann's e-mail address and signed off with "Good luck—you won't need it!" He expected that would be the last he'd hear of Shannon Hamilton. The potent feeling of control over the small mess he'd gotten himself into with Shannon was fleeting, supplanted by a worry and anxiety he hadn't known since leaving Arizona, since Olivia had packed her bags and flown out of his life.

He'd been unsettled by a chance encounter with Shelleyan, who had shrieked his name from across Union Square Park the day before. She'd dyed her hair a shiny chestnut color and had cut it at a severe angle. He hardly recognized her. "So there you are," she said. "I've been leaving messages for you." Charlie shrugged and moved down the sidewalk. Shelleyan kept stride. "Olivia is coming to New York," she announced theatrically. "I'm picking her up at the airport on Tuesday. She's going to stay with me. And I thought maybe we could all get together."

He mumbled an apology about being very busy.

"I've been temping at *Shout!*" she said. "Congrats on your story. You've come a long way in a short time."

The calculus whereby Shelleyan sneaked a copy of Charlie's story to Olivia, who had probably read it in disgust, was easy math. He was convinced that Olivia's sole motivation in coming to New York was to confront him about his fraudulent portrayal of their time together. As the crowds hustled around them, a thrumming in his head spread to the rest of his body. His nerves frenzied, as if Olivia might turn the corner and find him, exposed, caught on the verge of escape. He hadn't considered until that moment how much his scheming nourished him, and that her complete silence sustained the whole of his ambition to get her back. But Shelleyan's invitation threatened proximity, and proximity would only mean exposing his rapidly withering dreams. None of what he'd undertaken would mean anything to Olivia. Worse, he was clueless what her reaction would be upon learning of his last few months. He couldn't summon a response plausible enough to be Olivia's, one that could be ascribed solely to her and not to any one of the faceless strangers passing by. It was like they'd never met; she was a featureless ghost, and he searched his mind for any tangible proof that he'd ever known her. Even Shelleyan appeared unrecognizable; she bore a vague resemblance to the girl from a lost time who berated him for not knowing who Vernon Downs was, or that he was Olivia's favorite writer—insinuating there was a reservoir of things he didn't know and could never understand—but she was far removed from the tiny community college cafeteria thousands of miles away in Arizona where they'd once crossed paths, and it seemed preposterous to be standing on a sidewalk in New York, listening to her prattle on about reunion. A fleeting thought grew manifest within him: That his connection to the past was just his own fanciful imagination. The Kepharts, and the McCallahans, and the Alexander-Degners, the Wallaces, the Chandlers, and now Olivia. What he thought he knew about her—about any of them—was just pure invention.

....

"You have to call me *now*," Vernon's agent said after the beep. No "Hello," no "Hi, how are ya?" "I don't know why you're not answering the Vermont number you gave me, but the *Post* has something and we need to talk about it. Call me, Vernon. I'm serious."

Before Daar Baumann finished her message, Charlie was out the door, struggling with the buttons on his shirt as he called for the elevator. Christianna's door opened and she emerged dressed for an evening out. She sized him up, but before he could spit out Kline's name, she withdrew into her loft. The elevator sounded and he suffered the interminable ride to the lobby, rushing out of Summit Terrace for a cab that was about to pull away, his breath a hot smoke against the windows.

The *Post* offices were grungier than he'd expected. A gruff security guard he tried to finesse wouldn't let him pass, instead calling up to Kline to announce his arrival.

"This *is* a pleasure," Kline said, greeting him as the elevator opened on the sixth floor. The glass cubicles in the bull pen were occupied with interns and secretaries, none of whom paid any interest as Kline ushered them into his office, a cramped space cluttered with papers and Yankees memorabilia. "My favorite player," Kline said when he caught Charlie admiring a baseball signed by Mickey Mantle. "Kid had two bad legs and kept hitting. Amazing, no?"

He didn't answer, didn't know what Kline was referring to, didn't want to know.

"Have a seat," Kline said, indicating a ratty leather chair opposite his messy desk. "To what do I owe this visit?" he asked.

Kline's coyness riled him and Charlie struggled with his lines. He had choked back tears earlier in the cab when he imagined Vernon's irate reaction to Kline publishing whatever article he proposed to publish.

"How did you find out?" Charlie asked.

Kline put his hand on his heart. "Find out what?"

"C'mon." Charlie leaned forward in his chair, measuring his breath. "How'd you figure it out?" On the cab ride over, he had considered forsaking Vernon Downs entirely and bolting from New York, later presenting the episode as an anecdote that would maybe amaze Olivia. But he was curious about the publication of his story in *Shout!* and wasn't ready to submarine what might be a burgeoning literary career. Could he manage both? It all depended on Kline, to his supreme amazement.

"That you're not Vernon Downs?" Kline waved at someone passing outside the office. "I bumped into Vernon when I visited Christianna after the party. I was just playing my cards close."

Charlie exhaled. He'd underestimated Kline by disregarding him, and the penalty phase was about to commence. "What's the pot?" he asked.

Kline pitched forward. "You ever had a nemesis?" he asked.

A crowded field of faces from the past came to mind. "So?"

"Mine is another reporter—he prefers 'journalist,' excuse me. He was accepted at the more prestigious *J* school, works for a more prestigious paper, gets the plum assignments, on down the line." Kline's phone rang and he glanced at it. "I first heard about his writing an unauthorized biography of Downs from a mutual ex-girlfriend." He held up his hands. "I can't even verbalize that situation, but anyway, she told me and so I just showed up at his Christmas party. Did you know anyone can go? You don't have to be invited. If you know about it, you just go. Pretty remarkable for someone so mysterious. I knew the address from Christianna's sister, and it didn't take much investigation to uncover the when."

"Does Christianna know?" Charlie asked. The thought hadn't occurred to him until just that moment.

Kline shook his head. "I don't care about what you're up to with her," he said. "She'll never say anything to her sister, if that's your concern."

Charlie was unsure of his primary concern. "I still don't know what this is all about," he said, shifting.

Kline shoved a piece of paper across the desk. Charlie recognized it at once, the letter that had turned up innocently in Vernon's archives, a letter he guessed Vernon hadn't meant to keep.

"It's a copy," Kline said, warning in his voice.

Charlie reread the letter from Burton LaFarge, the accusation of plagiarism infinitely more menacing as he sat in Kline's office than it had been when he'd first discovered it in the safety of the loft. "Did you write this?" he asked, tossing the letter back across the desk. Stall, stall, stall.

"You know I didn't."

He thought of another tack: "How did you get it?" He guessed breaking and entering wasn't a talent Kline possessed.

"I told Christianna I could get her a couple of auditions," Kline said without a trace of chagrin. "She should take some acting lessons from you, though. That day at lunch? An amazing performance."

The emotional swing brought on by Christianna's betrayal was sickening. He'd never be able to explain to Olivia about why and how he'd come to New York and ended up embarrassing himself by pretending to be Vernon Downs. He wouldn't be able to use as an excuse how expert he'd become at pretending. It was all over if Kline printed what he knew. He began the cost-benefit analysis he'd employed in previous situations created out of his eagerness to fit in, or his yearning to be liked, measuring what had been forfeit against what could be revised in his favor, and he realized that the option to simply move on to the next thing, whatever it was, was his to exercise. Whatever mistakes or missteps he'd made in Denver, and Santa Fe, and Rapid City, San Diego, and Phoenix, had always accrued mercilessly until he'd wish for another move if only to wipe the slate clean.

But maybe it could all be salvaged, he thought. Perhaps Kline would barter the LaFarge letter for a raunchy tale about Jeremy Cyanin involving hookers and a substantial quantity of cocaine, insinuating that Cyanin was a bagman for a local crime family and that he might have participated in a hit. Or a believable story about Cyanin's sexual depravity, something involving ropes and turpentine, but that lie paled in comparison to Charlie's impersonating Vernon Downs, and the mental narrative he began to spin about Cyanin and the mob spiraled out of control and out of the realm of believability. He surrendered to his compromised position.

"What is it you want?" he asked.

The passing crowd barely registered as he exited the *Post* building, nearly tripping over a homeless woman squatting out on a flattened refrigerator box, Kline's outrageous request for access to Vernon's archives to write the better biography as the price of Kline's silence, both in the pages of the *Post* and with Christianna, ringing in his ears. Kline had pushed for Charlie's help in securing authorized status for the biography, but even Kline knew this was overreaching. Charlie assented to the request simply to win his freedom. Late-August humidity swarmed the city, the stink of garbage piled high on the sidewalk nauseating. Sweat trickled down his back as he waved in vain for a cab during rush hour.

....

The lock to Derwin's brownstone resisted Charlie's key. He leaned against the diamond-shaped window scarred by weather and vandalism and peered in, but the entryway was deserted.

"He died." Mrs. Cooper, the ancient Puerto Rican neighbor who could pass entire days loitering on her stoop, told about Derwin's fall, the ambulance that whisked him away, demolishing his summer plans for Fire Island and forever after. She couldn't answer Charlie's question about who changed the locks, but uttered something incomprehensible about Derwin's brother in Baltimore.

Charlie glanced up at his former residence, the tiny studio apartment sealed like a tomb. He felt the first tremors of hysteria as he grieved for what was lost, mostly the suede pouch from the Kepharts that held his valuables:

The aluminum diamonds from the long-ago Batman and Robin performance had traveled with him for so long they'd turned yellow. The skit had ended triumphantly, good finally trumping evil as Charlie skated across his homeroom floor, undercutting the Joker's legs so that the bag of foil diamonds soared, spraying the tiny silver jewels under the desks of their classmates, a choreographed move they'd practiced in the hall. George proudly wore the remnants of the white makeup used to paint him as the Joker that wouldn't wash off, the three of them accepting the wows of their peers, who they believed considered them superheroes. The Joker's capture and the players' ovation weren't the close of the drama for Charlie, however. The conclusion of the play would be asking Suzy Young to be his girlfriend. He'd chosen breakfast in the gymnasium as the venue for his proposal, but he waited a couple of days, allowing for the legend of the Batman and Robin skit to propagate, he imagined, before approaching Suzy. He'd purposely stayed clear of her to avoid losing his new sheen of celebrity, which was why he was oblivious about her father's abrupt transfer to Idaho, the reason Suzy was absent from breakfast on the day he'd hoped would be their happiest. Charlie frantically searched the gymnasium, asking her friends if they knew where she was. Suzy's desk remained empty during the morning classes, and he finally asked Mrs. Holstein about Suzy as the others filed out for recess, collapsing in tears when Mrs. Holstein told him the awful truth.

Gone too was the wedding ring Michelle Benson had given him in the fourth grade. Michelle's friends had been the inspiration to take the relationship to the next level. "Why don't you just ask her to marry you?" they chimed, a dare Charlie converted into proposal, asking Michelle if she would marry him in a note before lunch. Michelle gamely accepted, less flattered than amused, he thought—she was always more amused by him than anything else—though he was the last to know of her decision, since it was Wednesday, which meant boarding the bus that pulled up outside Mrs. Selby's class and honked in the middle of the day, Charlie the lone student from Lewis and Clark in the Gifted and Talented Program hosted by Webster Elementary. He bemoaned his showy cleverness at the annual spelling bee—he discovered an ability to spell words whose definitions eluded him—an exhibition that landed him in the gifted program. He dreaded Wednesdays, not because he sensed his classmates staring at him and his cumbersome backpack as he climbed onto the near-empty bus, or because he had to walk home alone from Webster through an unfamiliar neighborhood, but because of the menacing he and his fellow gifted students suffered on the Webster playground.

His enrollment in the gifted program was a source of tension in the McCallahan household, too: The McCallahans never asked him about it, and Wednesdays came and went like the other days of the week, so that it felt like Charlie's secret, a quiet he associated with the school nurse's diagnosis that Ian was dyslexic, though when Charlie overheard Mrs. McCallahan telling Mr. McCallahan, she said the word in a way that betrayed her disbelief in the nurse's medical qualifications. For his part, Ian never let on that the gifted program bothered him, though Ian barely came out of his room when Charlie knocked to say good-bye before being shipped out to Rapid City without a chance to properly divorce Michelle.

Charlie's wedding day was attended by most of the girls in his class. The event was booked for the early recess, near the monkey bars. One of

Michelle's friends made a crown for her to wear, and Charlie fashioned two rings out of twist ties. The ceremony was quick and consisted of Michelle and Charlie holding hands while they were pronounced man and wife by Michelle's best friend. "You may now kiss the bride," someone yelled, and he angled forward, Michelle taking the kiss on her cheek.

Lost was the letter from Ms. Slater, his first-grade teacher, her acknowledgment of the carefully wrapped package containing a necklace and a ring from the machine at the grocery store that spit out plastic bubbles full of wonderful prizes that he'd left on her chair the last day of class. Charlie would stare moon-eyed at Ms. Slater from his seat near the back of the room, listening but not listening to whatever subject they were studying. He didn't endeavor to impress her with his academic work; that route was too pedestrian. His own burgeoning affinity for the dramatic was born out of the anonymity that had claimed him since his parents died. Instead he chose "My Bonnie Lies over the Ocean" from the songbook his piano teacher had given him and practiced it incessantly, working for perfection, willing himself to tears on the refrain "Bring back my Bonnie to me." He dreamed of performing the ditty to a packed concert hall, smiling in Ms. Slater's direction after the touching performance, the only variation on the dream being the hairstyle Ms. Slater wore. The recital dream was so real he could summon its emotional aftershocks at will, reveling in it over and over so that the moment felt like a shared secret, an illicit romance his classmates were oblivious to. Worried that she'd forget him—and slightly paranoid that she'd vanish before the start of the next school year—he hoped the jewelry would serve as a reminder of his affection and that she'd look forward to seeing him as eagerly as he looked forward to seeing her in the fall. A tizzy threatened his summer until he found a letter addressed in Ms. Slater's hand:

Dear Charlie,

    I was so surprised to find a present on my desk after school. Thank you so much for the lovely necklace and ring.

I have been having a nice summer. Mostly I've just been lazy—doing a lot of reading and sunbathing. I have a new car and will probably be going on a trip later this summer. I plan to visit my sister in Spokane and my parents in Portland, and go to Seattle for the King Tut exhibit.

I hope your summer is a lot of fun.

Love,

Ms. Slater

He'd never again hold the Mormon dance card he'd acquired so that he could attend dances with Jenny, his high school girlfriend. His theory that Mormonism was the sole obstacle to a secure future with Jenny had been wrong. He guessed that swaying Jenny from Mormonism would be a nearly impossible task, but everything hinged on it, so when he read about a documentary proving conclusively that Mormonism was substantially make-believe, he perceived it as his last last chance. Jenny's letters from college had ceased leading up to Christmas, and he hoped her silence was simply reticence to engage his harangue that religion was just a form of governance, rather than a repudiation of him entirely.

Jenny's expression when she opened the door, the aroma of her family's dinner wafting in his direction, revealed how far he'd fallen. "This isn't a good time," she said, as if he were a salesman conniving for just one cup of coffee. Her expression contracted when she spotted the documentary he was cradling, tears streaming down his face. She'd already disowned him, he could see that, but the glint in her eye communicated how much his materializing with the anti-Mormon video violated the last sacrament between them—the remembrance of how much they'd once loved each other—rendering the memory impotent. Jenny's look hardened and Charlie divined the shattering news that he had been unaware of: She had moved on. A downdraft whipped through the yard and Jenny stepped away from the screen door. The sonorous vibration of laughter burst from the house, and Jenny glanced reflexively toward the dining room, the same dining room where he'd supped on numerous occasions, encircled in prayer around the polished table with Jenny and her family, giving thanks, Charlie finally drawn completely into the comfort of home. He stammered a valediction about his embarrassment at having interrupted dinner, but Jenny cut him off again with "This isn't a good time," and the expression he must've worn his first day in Denver, and Santa Fe, and Rapid City, and San Diego, and Phoenix—the look of someone who was starting over—spread across the constellation of freckles he used to spend afternoons counting with clandestine kisses. And although he'd worn the expression in countless circumstances, he'd never had to suffer it—he'd always been the one moving on, leaving friends and familiarity in his wake—and the effect was devastating. As Jenny closed the door, her silhouette rejoining the festivities, he stood in darkness, drowning in Jenny's disdain, his losses mounting, his eyes wet with regret.

Charlie turned his back on the brownstone and Mrs. Cooper, who had struck up a conversation with the girl from the corner Laundromat, out circling the block on her afternoon smoke break, and walked away. The initial exhilaration that visited him when a new chapter began predictably shaded into depression. Unlimited freedom didn't guarantee happiness, he knew firsthand, though it always promised it and he thirsted for that promise.

Charlie migrated unencumbered toward the subway, disguised in the crowd as somebody racing toward something. A swell of warm, recycled air escaped from somewhere deep underground as he paced the L platform, the launching point for whatever was next. He refused to acknowledge the emotional attrition invested in every next adventure, every new face, every new terrain.

"Who are you?" Kline had asked as Charlie stormed out of the *Post* offices, but Charlie had no answer.

IV

CHARLIE GRIPPED THE leather wheel of the black BMW, raindrops from the brief rainstorm as they crossed the border into Pennsylvania sparkling on the hood. The instrument panel cast an orange glow over Vernon's features as he slept coiled in the passenger seat. The lush green landscape darkened as the car raced west along the ribbon of wet highway. He'd had to force his way into the driver's seat in a showdown with Vernon in front of Summit Terrace. The days between Charlie's meeting with Kline and Vernon's frightening appearance had been filled with uncertainty about what exactly was next. He'd camped out at Vernon's, indiscriminately shoving the archives back into boxes, having unplugged the answering machine. Christianna's presence just beyond the lofts' common wall was felt but not seen, her betrayal enmeshed with that cancerous Kline, the hallway eerily quiet each time Charlie had food delivered. A low-level dread about Jessica appearing unannounced corrupted his sleep, so that a fogginess plagued him through the daylight hours as he tried to dream up a new scheme that would propel him to the next new world, wherever that was.

As the date of Olivia's arrival drew near, a series of bargaining positions hampered his ability to plan. He was convinced he was hanging around Vernon's loft, delaying, because he was going to keep the date with Olivia and Shelleyan, until he was doubly convinced that he would not, which made urgent an errand he'd been avoiding.

He'd been carrying the name Harold E. Turnbull around forever, since he noted the signature scrawled on the police report from that awful day. The police report judged his parents' death accidental, caused by a gas leak in the basement. Charlie knew the basement had filled with gas, and was made to understand it was the pilot light that had sent the house into orbit. When he subsequently secured a copy of the report by mail, he searched for clues that it could've been otherwise. Couldn't it have been some other type of accident? Couldn't there have been a defect in the hot-water heater? Wasn't there someone else who could share the blame? Would he have to wake with the same heavy sadness that put him to sleep night after night? As he grew older, he would toss in his tiny bed under the eaves of his aunt and uncle's soundless house, convinced that he'd seen a shadowy figure lurking that fateful day, though by morning he was always devastated by the awareness that it simply wasn't true.

Harold E. Turnbull lived on Mott Street in Chinatown; the computer in the New York Public Library had imparted this bit of information as easily as it churned out queries by subject, author, or title. Previously, he'd uncovered a rat's nest of Turnbulls in Minnesota, and he'd called every one, hoping for a relative. It wasn't until he found respite from the oppressive summer heat at the New York Public Library that he even thought to try New York, or anywhere east of the Mississippi, for that matter. And there he was, residing on Mott Street the whole time, waiting for him. Harold E. Turnbull. Of Mott Street. New York, New York. He wondered what sort of person Harold E. Turnbull was: Did he have a family? Was he from California? Had he ever before seen a house reduced to sticks and scraps of metal, the occupants of the house gone, gone, gone—gone into the atmosphere?

Mott Street wasn't any wider than an alley, and the cab cruised slowly, the cabbie scanning for the address. The car halted and Charlie paid the fare and stood alone in front of a dark building appointed with a gray door. His hand shook as he pressed the button under the name H. E. TURNBULL. A husky voice answered: "Yes?"

He didn't know this part of it. He barely knew what he would say when he got into Harold Turnbull's apartment, much less how to gain entrance. "You don't know me, Mr. Turnbull," he said, "but I've come to speak to you. It's about my parents."

"Hello?" the husky voice asked again.

Charlie cleared his throat and started again. "I've come to—"

"Hello? Who is it? Hello?" the voice barked, and then clicked off. Charlie's heart sank, and he searched the shadowed street for a pay phone—he'd copied Harold Turnbull's phone number, too, and would try to call and explain—but he managed only two steps before the door buzzed, and he pushed it, slamming it against the wall. The door caught and closed slowly as a trapezoid of plaster plummeted to the floor.

Charlie used the handrail to navigate the unlit stairway to the fourth floor. The door to Harold Turnbull's apartment strained against the gold chain, and a set of owl eyes blinked out from behind a pair of enormous spectacles.

"Hello? What do you want?"

Charlie stood back, not wanting to distress his prey. "I think you knew my parents," he said, choosing an expediency rooted in truth. "In Modesto. It was a long time ago. You were the city inspector there, right?" He flinched when the door swung open. The smell of ripe bananas escaped the apartment.

"It's nice to have a visitor," Turnbull said. Charlie figured him to be about seventy-five, but it was impossible to tell because his loose flesh and bald head gave him the appearance of having been dead for a long time, resurrected only by Charlie's visit.

The tiny apartment was cluttered with unread newspapers, some still in their plastic sheaths. Empty orange juice cartons were stashed behind the recliner positioned directly in front of the television. A dozen or so chocolate bars were spilled across the tiny black-and-gray-flecked Formica kitchen table. A familiar scene from an old sitcom squawked from the television and they both stood and stared at it.

"I'll clear this away," Turnbull said. A foul odor emanated as he swept a rack's worth of bundled magazines off a ragged couch.

Charlie lost his nerve. What if Turnbull looked at him and said, "Yes, it was your fault"? What if he said, "If you and your friend hadn't been fucking around in the basement, your parents would still be alive today"? It hadn't occurred to him that the only reason he'd sought out Harold Turnbull was that he wanted absolution, to have him testify it was an accident, that it might've been something else, anything—a meteor falling out of the sky, a bomb planted by terrorists, a rocket mistakenly fired from the local army base.

Turnbull plunked into the recliner and elevated his feet. "Circulation," he said, wincing. "Now, what is this all about?"

Charlie fingered an imaginary spot on his pants. He felt Turnbull staring over his socked toes at him, and he summoned the Olympic courage he sometimes willed to power him through situations that he'd misjudged as easy but that proved surprisingly difficult. He told Turnbull about that day when he was seven, about him and his sixteen-year-old sitter, the neighbor girl, Kyra, roller-skating in the basement—it was safer than the street, where a car could roar around the corner and kill you dead just like that. It was his mother who had suggested it, actually. "Why don't you go down in the basement if you want to skate," she'd said. Charlie wouldn't have come up with that idea in a million years, as appealing as it was. He told Turnbull about coming home later from the store, Kyra in tow, and discovering a gap of sunlight where his house had stood. He confessed how he sometimes saw the house in his dreams. Not the same exact house; sometimes it was red or green or blue, sometimes a single-story ranch, but no matter what color or shape, he always recognized it as his childhood home, the house disintegrating into colored confetti when he turned the brass knob.

"Very interesting," Turnbull said.

"And so," Charlie said, weary from the effort it took to expel the story he'd secreted away for most of his life, "I just need to know if you think what happened that day might have been an accident."

Turnbull removed his glasses and pinched the bridge of his nose. "It was a lifetime ago," he said.

"I brought this," Charlie said, handing him the yellowed copy of the police report.

Turnbull held his glasses aloft, inspecting the document. "That's my signature, all right," he said. Charlie inched forward on the couch. He'd grown accustomed to the stench in the apartment. "The thing is . . . it was a lifetime ago."

"Are you saying you don't remember?" Charlie asked. "How many houses have you seen blown to pieces?"

"Just hold on," Turnbull said. He kicked himself out of the chair and handed back the report. "Let me just—would you like a drink? I find a drink sometimes helps."

Charlie demurred. His heart was pounding. Turnbull poured himself two fingers of bourbon and flushed it down. He poured another glassful and returned to the recliner. Outside, a siren wailed and Turnbull's apartment was briefly flooded with emergency.

"Were your neighbors affected?" he asked.

The question staggered him. His memories of that terrible day and since had never accounted for the neighbors, and he strained to conjure any details about them. The one across the street had maybe been a dentist, and he definitely remembered a patch of sunflowers in the yard adjacent to his, the sunflowers coming into view when he and Kyra kicked higher and higher on the plastic swing set his father had staked to the ground with metal chains the previous Christmas. But he couldn't be certain. His neighbors in Denver had had sunflowers, and it was conceivable the dentist had actually lived opposite him in Santa Fe. A flush of embarrassment overcame him, dubious about whether Turnbull was chastising him for his self-absorption, or whether a detail or two about those who lived on his childhood street in California would really help spur his memory. The conceit that his neighbors, whoever they were, had carried on with their lives after his house had immolated seemed incredible—the street had assumed the form of a tableau in Charlie's mind, untroubled by the present or future—and triggered the discomforting thought that someone had more than likely built a house on the ruins of his parents' house, a sacrilege that he'd never considered. Did Kyra still live in the neighborhood? Why hadn't he wondered that before? Maybe Kyra was keeping his memory alive on that tiny street. Maybe she wondered what had become of him, and he was startled at how powerful the feeling was.

"What do you want me to say?" Turnbull asked. "Do you want me to say it wasn't an accident? How could it be anything else?" He took another swig of bourbon. "Do you want me to exonerate you, assure you that you were not the cause of the accident?"

Charlie didn't respond.

"Well," Turnbull said, "maybe. Maybe the leak was caused by something else. Maybe it wasn't a leak at all—hell, back in those days if a house blew up, we *assumed* it was a gas leak. We couldn't do what they can do now." He finished the second glass of bourbon. "I will tell you this," he said. "Accidents happen and sometimes they change your life, but they're still accidents. You shouldn't try to look for meaning in them. An accident is an accident."

Turnbull sat back in the recliner. Charlie tucked away the photocopy of the police report. He thanked Turnbull for his time, but Turnbull started to snore loudly, so he let himself out. Something had just happened—he felt it—but what? Had anything Turnbull said made any difference, or was he saying that nothing anyone could say would make a difference, and by extension, that the past was the past and had no bearing on the present or the future? It was a homily he had trouble believing. The sun was starting to set on Mott Street, and Charlie fruitlessly hailed a cab, somehow sorry that he'd finally found Harold E. Turnbull, the years of hope and comfort he'd derived from the name whisked away on a hot afternoon wind of regret.

The visit to Turnbull had been so taxing and left him so rent he failed to make it to the lobby to collect the mail, the annoyed doorman delivering it one afternoon wrapped with a thick rubber band. Among the mail was the unopened apology he'd mailed to the famous author Vernon had quarreled with, marked UNDELIVERABLE. He opened the letter and was reading the heartfelt apology when a disheveled Vernon Downs appeared, his hair matted to his head as if it were raining, his normally smooth face unshaven, a barbaric spark in his eyes. Charlie had girded against rebuke, but Vernon muttered something about California, his words slurring as he grabbed random articles from the loft and deposited them into paper shopping bags, Charlie revolving around him silently, the two pirouetting through the unkempt loft until Vernon hefted the two bags by their handles and stalked toward the door. The rush of excuses that had flooded Charlie's brain when Vernon appeared evaporated, and without being asked, he followed Vernon down the emergency stairs to the street where the BMW languished amid the cacophony of honking cabs and animated, competitive sidewalk conversations. Vernon dropped the shopping bags in the backseat on top of his luggage from Vermont. After a confused moment where Vernon begged to drive to calm himself, Charlie slipped behind the wheel and listened to Vernon's harangue against his editor, who had driven him to the fringes of madness over the latest revision of the new novel, punctuated by directions on how to flee the city by car.

"'Make it more Vernon Downs–y,'" Vernon repeated incredulously, his eyes bulging, his breath stale from cigarettes. "What does he know about it?" he asked angrily. "Take the George Washington Bridge." Charlie followed Vernon's directions, Manhattan slowly receding, the skyline shrinking into miniature. "What does anyone know about it?" Vernon asked softly.

"What did the editor mean?" Charlie asked.

Vernon cracked the window and lit a cigarette. "It's a tired impression at this point, is all," was the answer. "You take what they give you and you burnish it, indulging it even," he said, "and then you realize you're in a prison of your own construction. I mean, I let it happen. This unrecognizable person in the papers was infinitely more interesting than I was. I'd read what they wrote about me and aspire to their interpretation. That was my mistake. I didn't understand how important it was to control your own narrative.

"I remember when I first learned *Minus Numbers* was going to be published, I was elated that something I'd dreamed up was going to find its way into print. That was it"—he exhaled through the open window— "but everything after that got . . . easier. I struggled and worried and fussed with *Minus Numbers*, and after it was published, I swear I could've published an annotated grocery list and it would've gotten the same reception as the books I did publish. You want to know why? Because the machinery was already in place to dictate the outcome. You're young, you write a book, you become famous, maybe make some money, which unleashes praise and jealousy in equal measure. So from then on out, a certain number of people worship you and a certain number of people loathe you. It's a mirror of everyone's life, just played out in the press." Vernon stubbed the cigarette out in the ashtray, where it smoldered among a salad of empty candy wrappers. "You once asked me what the most untrue thing anyone ever said about me was. 'Controversial and reclusive East Coast literary novelist.' The person who first coined it should've trademarked it. If words were money, that person would be rich beyond rich. Ask anyone, there's nothing controversial about me personally. You see something, you translate it into words and create *fictional* characters to generate meaning, and then you're liable for these things that you simply witnessed and recorded. And they call you reclusive if you don't want to answer questions asked by someone who either hasn't read the work or wants to confuse your characters with you. And worse: You take the bait and start equivocating on earlier denials that your work is any kind of reflection on your life. You have some fun blurring the edges, fanning the embers of the secret desires people who hardly know you harbor. Disappearance is the only remedy. What other answer is there? I'm forced to disappear if I want to wake up and live the way I was before *Minus Numbers* and everything else. I can't go back to New York. There's no peace in New York."

Vernon had leaned against the window as he rambled on about the ways his self-impersonation had gone astray, how he had allowed what was said about him to inform his perception of himself, how he had acted his way through life accordingly. He fell silent and Charlie assumed he'd finally dozed off. "Against all my better instincts, I went to the tenth anniversary of Nell's," Vernon said, barely audible, his voice shot through with sadness. "I went there very early with a friend of mine; we thought we'd have a glass of champagne and it would be like the Haunted Mansion at Disneyland. I hadn't been there in five years, and we realized it would be really scary but we had to do it. We had spent so much time hanging out there with so many. It was really at one point the nexus of publishing. It was the hub of where everyone who was involved with publishing in New York would hang out. So we walk in and we sit in the same booth we always sat in whenever we were there, and then we noticed that a couple of us were drinking Diet Cokes, people were smoking light cigarettes, no one was doing blow on the table, everyone was checking their watch. Basically we all felt really old. Everyone was controlled by how manic the times were, which sort of demanded that you rush out to every restaurant you possibly could, party with every famous person you possibly could, buy everything you read about in magazines, act this way, look this way, do this."

Vernon's monologue saturated Charlie's mind as he struggled against the monotony of the road. He resisted Vernon's interpretation, ascribing it to fatigue and a toxic moroseness induced by whatever had happened in Vermont. He guessed Jacqueline Turner and the other authors gathered at Bemelmans on that not-so-long-ago afternoon would've traded some privacy for an ounce of Vernon's exposure. Everything had a price, he knew well, and it was either paid voluntarily or forcefully extracted. Still, Vernon's madness was real. They were on their way to California, to his mother's house in Los Angeles. That was real. He wondered at Vernon's game plan for a second act in L.A. Perhaps it was just to be closer to friends and family. But his money would run out eventually. Vernon's celebrity would hamper his ability to interview for the variety of jobs people held to pay their bills, much like Charlie's own resume, which was largely a chronology of absence.

"You never said where you were from," Vernon said, yawning. "With most people . . . it comes up." Vernon yawned again. "Just stay on the I-80 West."

Charlie struggled with the question, rescued by a suite of sighs that preceded a light, melodious snoring. A calm settled over him as the extent of his liberation unfolded. Kline's demands, the drama with Christianna, the threat of reunion with Olivia with Shelleyan as witness—all erased. Like in Denver, when he'd forsaken Jesse Mason's friendship after the Batman and Robin skit to throw his lot in with a group of popular kids, a transition Jesse's mother and Mrs. Kephart ignored as Jesse's birthday party loomed, the awkwardness aborted when Charlie landed with the McCallahans, who were ignorant of the drama involving Michelle Benson. Not his pretend nuptials, but that after a brief acrimony toward the boyfriend she'd broken up with to be with him, he and the ex-boyfriend became friends, to Michelle's chagrin. Charlie eventually spent more time with the ex-boyfriend than he did with Michelle, and soon they were distributing He-Man Michelle Haters Club cards they'd printed on the ex-boyfriend's home computer. He recoiled when he thought about how easily he adopted the manners and interests of others as a coping mechanism for always being the new kid in the new school. He still didn't drink orange soda because Michelle hated it; he adopted Jesse Mason's opinion that the moon landing had been faked, something Jesse's parents had told him. He became a Vernon Downs fan because of Olivia. He could think of endless examples. Vernon had liberated him from the mess back in New York like his move from San Diego to Phoenix had freed him from academic embarrassment, his short tenure as Miss Wade's student aide. His chemistry teacher's initial attentiveness was flattering, and he held the position with a pridefulness that other students must've found distasteful. But when he began to hear whispers that Miss Wade was a motorcycle-riding lesbian—rumors that were never confirmed—his attitude underwent a transformation, and it wasn't long before he was leaking the answers to Miss Wade's exams to anyone who asked, which was briefly a fountain of popularity. Miss Wade quickly discovered the hustle when the exact sequence of correct multiple choice answers were applied to an alternate test she'd utilized so that students couldn't pass answers from class to class. Charlie's demotion to study hall wasn't as perilous as the ire of the student body, and he was mulling begging the Wallaces to allow him to transfer high schools when he was shipped out again, to Phoenix, the immediate threat ameliorated just like that. Same for the trouble he'd gotten into with some classmates the summer of his junior year at Randolph Prep; the emancipation the Chandlers helped him engineer bailed him out of having to testify to the administration about how the fellowship at Garden Lakes, a sort of summer camp, had gone awry.

He slowed as the night sky colored red and orange, the taillights of the cars ahead of them flaring. The nose of the BMW almost kissed the bumper sticker on a yellow VW that read, IF YOU WERE AN AIRLINE PILOT, WE'D ALL BE DEAD. Charlie obsessed over all its meanings as the line of cars snaked forward in the dark. Vernon shifted in the passenger seat, his sleep cycle unbroken. The car at rest, and without the lullaby of the tires on the road, Charlie was wide awake. A police cruiser with its lights flashing passed silently on the shoulder, followed by an ambulance. He wondered idly if the driver of the yellow VW was embarrassed about the bumper sticker in this instance, when it could be that someone did actually die, and possibly due to poor decision making. Or did the driver even remember that the bumper sticker was there? Charlie could envision a scenario where the driver slapped it on, as either a statement or a joke, and then quickly forgot about it, maybe only remembering it when he noticed it, or if someone asked him about it, where they could get one too. The bumper sticker morphed into a provocation as Charlie was compelled to stare at it when traffic came to a standstill. The deep woods on either side of the interstate bred a claustrophobia he attempted to abate by turning on the air conditioner. The slight breeze simulated enough movement to quell the aggravating implication that Charlie was as disconnected from his various experiences as the driver was from the bumper sticker on his car. It had meant something to him once, but he barely considered it now. To his relief, the yellow VW put on its flashers and pulled over to the side of the road. As he passed, Charlie smiled at the driver, a bearded man in his fifties who jumped out and popped his trunk.

By sunrise, they were well into Ohio. Charlie had stopped to relieve himself and fill the tank, waving the Speedpass on Vernon's key chain at the Exxon station off I-80 as Vernon slept in the passenger seat. When he finally awoke, just past Springfield, he said, "Take I-75 South," and they veered off the exit, headed for Cincinnati. Without inquiry, Vernon gave a thumbnail account of the reason for their detour: that his ex-wife, Jayne, and nine-year-old son, Robby, lived in Blue Ash, a suburb just outside Cincinnati. Charlie absorbed the facts, that Vernon had met Jayne when she was a model in New York, right after he'd published *Scavengers*, that they had had a long, protracted battle involving private detectives over Vernon's paternity—"We kept calling each other John and Jane Doe after it was finally resolved," Vernon said—followed by a quick marriage that lasted a mere three months. After a quiet divorce, Jayne had moved to Blue Ash and made Vernon swear not to utter a word about them as he went on with his life. "Not for their own privacy," he said, "but because I'm an embarrassment as a father and ex-husband." The story staggered Charlie, as did Vernon's ability to keep it out of his official biography.

The modest white and blue ranch house on Laurel Avenue was shrouded behind clouds of hydrangeas. A red Jeep Cherokee sat in the driveway, the back passenger door inexplicably left open. Vernon stared uneasily at the open car door, perhaps sensing the visit was a mistake, the signs of apology troubling his brow. He fortified himself with the last of the cigarettes that had substituted for his breakfast. A golden retriever bounded across the lawn toward the Cherokee. "Victor," Vernon said. "That dog hates me." Charlie braced for Vernon to make the connection between the golden retriever and Oscar—Vernon had amnesia about the missing dog—but Oscar had apparently been consigned to the past, just as Jessica predicted.

A slender woman in blue jeans and a yellow sheer chiffon button-front blouse appeared in the driveway, shading her eyes. Her long black hair fluttered in the morning breeze. Vernon stepped out of the BMW and waved. The woman lowered her hands and retreated inside. Vernon leaned into the car. "Come back tomorrow," he said, shutting the door and sauntering across the thick grass. The golden retriever ran aimlessly toward him and then pulled up, changing direction and jogging ahead of Vernon toward the front door.

The separation caused Charlie a moment of panic, which quickly converted to anger at being abandoned. Regardless of his intellectual preparedness, it was always a wonderment, that first prick of panic and then the wall of anger that rendered him powerless until he could hack through his emotions to take inventory of his new circumstances, which would reveal what would be required of him to survive. In the case of Vernon's precipitous exit, the primary concern was that he'd be obliged to sleep in the BMW, his funds mostly depleted from his summer in Manhattan. As he cruised the quiet suburban streets, idly guessing at what it would be like to grow up in the bucolic heaven that was Blue Ash, he scouted for camouflage, which would only need to hold until tomorrow morning, when he could legitimately go for breakfast, or find a bookstore to satisfy his curiosity about whether the good citizens of Middle America read Vernon Downs. But after unsuccessfully trolling the local radio station for a soundtrack to his latest dilemma, Charlie fished for a CD in the leather armrest and discovered a stash of twenties he hoped Vernon wouldn't remember. A quick alibi—that he'd used the money to gas up in Pennsylvania—would be believable until Vernon received the bill for his Speedpass, at which point Charlie guessed it wouldn't be an issue. His cover story thus salted away, he rented an antiseptic room at a Motel 6 and fell on the blue and green checkered comforter in his clothes, staring at the television to dull his mind of all that had transpired.

He awoke after midnight, restless. The Motel 6 complex was a hulking ghost ship in a sea of suburban sprawl. The warm August night draped the landscape in a purple bloom, specks of headlights roving in the distance. The vending machine in the concrete courtyard swallowed Charlie's quarters without reciprocation. He pummeled the glass, but the Hostess cupcakes slumbered behind their wire guard. He unsuccessfully rummaged the BMW for more change, though his hunger ebbed when he discovered a cardboard box stashed under Vernon's luggage containing typewritten pages, the new novel. Charlie turned the pages carefully, sprawled out on the sheets back in his room. The novel was without a title page but involved several characters from Vernon's second novel, *Scavengers*, many of whom had gone on to become models. The narrator shared the same name as the golden retriever, and he chuckled at the connection. As he read, the narrative became a hybrid of satire and thriller, involving models as terrorists, the overt thesis intimating the tyranny of beauty.

Charlie set the pages aside. The myth of Vernon Downs—even after it had been punctured by the madness that had them scampering across the country—was so ingrained in his mind, so saturated in association to bygone days with Olivia in Phoenix, that he was incapable of judging if the book was any good. Were reviewers right about Vernon? Was he a hack, a sensationalist, a writer more famous for being famous than for being a writer? He recalled a scurrilous accusation he'd read somewhere—that if not for the controversy surrounding *The Vegetable King*, Vernon would still be published by his original publisher, whose reputation as a purveyor of celebrity biographies and gimmicky books had been cemented in recent years. Regardless, however the new novel turned out, it would be published, a record of Vernon's particular interests and thoughts at a certain time in his life. The book would be a written record, a permanence in an otherwise transitory existence, and Charlie traced his attraction to writing back through his want for a little attention to this lust for immortality. If only he could bead his experiences on a chain, not just to memorialize them in print for posterity, but to search them for threads of meaning or instructive themes.

The sun ascended in the milky sky, the beginning of another humid summer day. Charlie checked out, too early to arrive at Vernon's ex-wife's place. His restlessness from the night before had ripened into a full-blown anxiety, a wariness that Vernon's visit with his ex would have them reversing course, back to New York. He slowly drove the streets of Blue Ash while its residents awoke. Without any concrete evidence to support his theory, he surmised that Blue Ash closely paralleled the neighborhood in Modesto where he'd lived with his parents, who had, over the years, become little more than a fact. He'd had parents, like everyone. But because both his mother and father had been substantially younger than their siblings, and had never been close with the kin who tended him, Charlie had left his biological family without any memento or recollection of them. His features were too ordinary and symmetrical to provide a sketch of familial resemblance, and without that mental purchase, he was helpless to speculate about what kind of people they were, if they subscribed to the tenets of religion and politics that most employed to define themselves, if they were college educated, if they were employed, if they were liked by their neighbors, if they saw people socially, if they were involved in neigh-

borhood concerns, if they ate regularly at local restaurants, liked spicy food
or unusual pizza toppings, if others recognized and regarded them when
they walked down the street, if they were more likely to dispense wisdom
or seek advice, if they paid their bills on time or pleaded for extensions, if
they happily agreed with taxes for community improvement or resented the
governmental intrusion on their personal finances, if they were progressive
or given to bouts of racism and sexism, if they were inclined to help someone
in need or pass by quickly, pretending not to see, if they liked pop music, if
they went to the movies regularly, followed sports, if they had the newspaper
delivered to the house or bought it occasionally, if they read books, listened
to talk radio, if they drove a new car or a used one, if they rented or owned
their home, if they had planned to save money for his college education, if
they showered him with kisses or treated him like they would an adult, if
they assiduously researched the quality of the local school system or not, if
they harbored secret crushes on neighbors or coworkers, if they drank coffee
or tea, if they were vegetarians, if they smoked, if they were afraid to fly, if
they had a history of cancer, if they feared technology, or nuclear war, if they
would've been the kind of parents he was proud or ashamed of, if he would've
forsaken them for adventure or stayed close as he grew older, if he would've
been closer to his mother or father, if he would've begged them for a sibling
or basked in the attention of being an only child, if he would have made them
proud or been the cause of disappointment, if they would've boasted about
him to friends and neighbors or been bound to shake their head with chagrin, if they would've been a close-knit family that took vacations together,
celebrated all the important holidays, and been devastated when one of them
was grievously injured or gravely ill, rendered inconsolable by death.

He wished he could know.

....

Vernon appeared rejuvenated by his overnight visit. His clothes
had been laundered, and a shower had all but resurrected his previously

beleaguered form. But Charlie noted that neither his ex nor the boy accompanied him to the car. Vernon motioned that he wanted to drive, so Charlie dutifully crawled into the passenger seat. They slipped back onto the freeway in silence, Vernon making lane changes without utilizing any mirrors or looking over his shoulder. He wasn't concerned about where Charlie had spent the night, or how he'd occupied himself during the gulf of time he'd been abandoned, and so Charlie stared out the window until he nodded off.

Vernon insisted on driving the rest of the way, darting off the freeway somewhere in Illinois, telling Charlie to stay in the car as they pulled up to a white clapboard house perched on a hill. The name carved in relief on the wooden sign in the shape of a tractor posted in the small garden out front—McInnis—was that of Vernon's onetime mentor at Camden. Vernon shook hands with the tall, gray-haired Harrison McInnis, who invited him in. Charlie reclined the seat, the BMW's air-conditioning vanquishing the first signs of heat. The cool, quiet chamber was broken moments later as Vernon climbed in, sweat on his forehead, his hair tousled and a sunburst-patterned red mark on his right cheek.

"We're off," he said, making a U-turn for the freeway.

"What happened?" Charlie asked.

"Just saying hello to an old friend," he answered.

Somewhere between the two Kansas Cities, Vernon fished a pill bottle out of his luggage and intermittently chewed small white tablets as they screamed across the Kansas plain, the darkness as pure as any Charlie had ever witnessed. The lone incandescent lights from gas stations and forlorn strip malls flashed by at metronomic intervals and Charlie fought sleep. Vernon cracked his window and increased the volume on the Stone Roses CD they'd listened to three times through. Conversation had been sparse, constrained to where to stop for fast food and gas, Vernon preoccupied with a point somewhere far along the horizon. Along a particularly endless expanse of pavement, the trance was snapped and the BMW eased to the shoulder.

"Christ," Vernon exhaled. He leaned his forehead on the steering wheel, completely deflated.

"I can get us to Denver," Charlie volunteered, and they wordlessly switched places, a tractor trailer blowing a torrid exhaust giving them a wide berth.

Charlie was so consumed by an intricate design whereby he might ditch Vernon at the hotel in Denver to surprise the Kepharts, the grandparents he hadn't seen or heard from in years, that he couldn't fathom the maze of one-way streets that would bring them to the towering chain hotel Vernon had pointed to, demanding sleep. The hotel mocked him as it drew near and then receded, none of the streets seemingly the answer to the riddle. "I thought you said you used to live here," Vernon said. Just when frustration threatened to flow like lava between them, the hotel's portico appeared. Vernon heaved his bag and disappeared through the electronic sliding doors while Charlie parked. Vernon's mental state made it impossible to predict how he'd react to the idea of borrowing money for a hotel room, so Charlie used the pay phone in the hotel lobby to call American Express to ask for a limit increase. He'd prepared a spurious anecdote about how he was starting a new job soon that would significantly boost his previously insubstantial income. The joyless voice denied the request, so Charlie climbed into the backseat of the BMW and rested his weary body on the leather seat. His head buzzed with thoughts of the Kepharts, replaced with a worry that they'd be disappointed to see him now, to know anything about what had happened to him since he left. He preferred they remember him as the little boy they'd briefly known so long ago.

....

Vernon appeared to believe the staged drama in the lobby about how Charlie had already checked out and was impatient to light out, and so the road trip recommenced, Vernon behind the wheel and Charlie the passen-

ger. Charlie tongued the hole in his back tooth where the temporary filling had been. He must've swallowed it in his sleep. The tooth would likely
weaken from infection before he could manage a way to fix it, he thought.

The blue snowcapped mountains disappeared as they crossed into
Utah, plunging into valleys of red rock, the arid landscape reminding
Charlie of his proximity to Arizona, a place he was sure he'd left for good.
The overnight stop in Denver and the sojourn through the desert southwest confirmed that the geographical backdrops of his personal history
continued to exist into the future, even though for Charlie they were frozen in amber, the glass bottles glinting in the sunshine of his mind. A
secondary thought, about the historical supposition about heading west in
search of a better life, or to make something of yourself, appeared as false
as anything.

As they skirted Las Vegas, Vernon regaled Charlie with the amusing
anecdote about how when he was in high school, his parents discovered
drugs in his room—"My sisters ratted me out!"—and they sent him to
work in his uncle's casino outside Vegas, forgetting that he'd mentioned it
previously in the interview, their first encounter, which seemed to Charlie
like several lifetimes ago.

A calmness descended on Vernon as they merged off the I-15 and
onto the I-10, passing signs for Pomona, West Covina, El Monte, and
Monterey Park, the locales sounding to Charlie as exotic as foreign coun-
tries. A bronze minivan and a blue Camaro, both with Michigan plates,
tried not to lose each other in traffic. A silver pickup truck changed lanes,
momentarily separating the two vehicles. Charlie watched with interest
as the minivan slowed to force the pickup truck to pass, reuniting the van
with the Camaro. He thought about the drivers planning for just such a
problem, devising the stratagem to protect each other all the way from
Michigan.

"I was born in Modesto," Charlie said between songs on the radio.

"Northern California is a whole different thing," Vernon said. "It's

Oregon, basically." His mood brightened as they broached the Los Angeles city limits. "I haven't been back in forever," he admitted. "Everyone out here calls me Dave. Harrison McInnis made me put my full name on the manuscript of *Minus Numbers* before he sent it to his agent. But I'm known to my real friends and family as Dave. I guess that punctures any remaining fiction about Vernon David Downs," he laughed. He stopped for a red light. "The myth is useful for a whole bunch of things, but it's a bummer when people buy into it too heavily. Like you did." He turned and looked at Charlie, who was processing the revelation, counting up the myths he'd adhered to for so long, a life with Olivia as rescue from his life of spirals overshadowing the rest of the list. "Hopefully you'll find something that means more to you than my literary facade." The light changed to green and the BMW rolled forward. "Unfortunately for me, I'm addicted to the fictional me," he added. Charlie took the admission to be Vernon's way of saying that he would ultimately return to New York and resume the life he'd fled a few days earlier. Charlie envied him the easy cover his image provided, in spite of its hazards and occasional nuisances.

They exited the freeway near Century City and headed toward Beverly Hills. "My father had an office in Century City," Vernon said. He spun a narrative about his previous life in Los Angeles, growing up in a pink stucco house on Valley Vista in Sherman Oaks, hanging out in Westwood at a Fatburger, the restaurant on Melrose where he used to have drinks with his mother, mobbing the twenty-four-hour Du-par's in Studio City, or Pages in Encino if Du-par's was packed. Vernon made a sequence of turns and noted how he used to wait patiently at the bar at La Scala Boutique, eating chopped salad and bribing the waitress to bring him red wine while his sisters shopped with their father's platinum AmEx card. "You used to go to La Scala Boutique to dodge the people who went to La Scala," he laughed, "which is impossible now, I'm sure." They passed a restaurant called Chasen's and Vernon said, "Christmas with the family there every year." Charlie admired the recitation, the parsing of Vernon's personal narrative, indifferent to the landmarks, which meant nothing to him. Only the Hollywood sign was familiar, but they motored under it without comment. "There used to be a yellow train on Sunset," Vernon lamented. In the middle of a story told with incredulity about how his parents had taken him to a place called Sambo's in Westwood when he was a kid, he broke off to ask, "Is today Sunday?"

Charlie wasn't sure, and said so, but Vernon became convinced and they drifted through the streets. The sky had been darkening all afternoon, the sun fighting through at intervals, the momentary brightness fouled by the thunderclouds approaching from the west. The Santa Monica Pier came into view, lit green and yellow and red against the black sky.

"We used to come down here on Sundays," Vernon said excitedly. "The last time I visited, I was shocked that people from my high school were keeping the tradition alive."

An exodus for cover was taking place as they pulled into a parking spot. Lightning streaked the sky, a sonorous crackle following. The ocean frothed, expelling the last swimmers. Vernon stood atop a pylon and shielded his eyes. "They're here somewhere," he said.

Charlie hoisted his duffel from the car as Vernon jogged down the dark beach. The car alarm engaged as he shut the door, and he was filled with wistfulness for the safe interior of the BMW, like driving by the home you were born in, knowing you would never live there again. He shouldered the bag and watched as Vernon receded into blackness, a web of lightning illuminating his outline, the lone figure marching toward the ocean while others ran for cover.

As Charlie moved inland, a light rain began to fall, the menace of a downpour in the air. He made for the taillights of a city bus as it pulled away from its stop, waving for the driver to stop, but the bus roared away. He'd hardly stepped into the shelter of the bus stop when the sky unburdened itself, unleashing a torrent that bathed the streets, rain bouncing off the hardened ground. He wondered if Vernon was looking for him, or if he'd turned to introduce him to his friends and shrugged when he found Charlie had disappeared. Neither really mattered. Either Vernon did or he didn't, and the consequences were the same to Charlie. Vernon wouldn't be surprised either way. He was right: Charlie had invested too much in Vernon's myth—they both had. Charlie often thought of his lack of a belief system—in anything—as a handicap, but wasn't life just a series of beliefs that mostly turned out not to be true? Or as true as you needed them to be? Wasn't the need to believe more interesting than the belief itself? In a sense, each new beginning in his life had been a rebirth, another chance. So many rebirths annihilated any thought of death, allowing recklessness to become his guiding principle.

"No more buses," someone shouted over the din of the hard rain, a vagrant taking refuge.

"No more buses?" Charlie repeated.

"Tomorrow is Labor Day," the vagrant said.

Charlie remembered the time he'd tried to take Olivia out to dinner for her birthday only to find all the restaurants closed on account of Thanksgiving, a fact they discovered after driving from restaurant to restaurant, playfully bargaining about the types of food they were willing to eat as they encountered each closed establishment, until they darted around Phoenix trying to locate a fast-food drive-through that was open.

"How could you not know it was Thanksgiving?" Olivia had asked. "Isn't it one of your biggest holidays?" He failed to explain that Thanksgiving was mostly a gathering of family and served no purpose for those who had grown up in a procession of tribal communities.

He smiled at the memory as the rivulets of rain collected in small tributaries. He wasn't devastated by Olivia or any of it, his ability to tie things off a skill he assumed most people would admire as they became bogged down by the minutiae of their lives. Back in New York, Christianna's sister was likely returning from Paris, ending Christianna's summer sublet. And Olivia and Shelleyan were probably strolling around Manhattan, Shelleyan relating what she knew about Charlie and his time in New York, which wouldn't amount to anything. The week before Vernon reappeared had been fraught with anxiety, and a small part of him was disappointed that he wasn't going to be called to account. Olivia meant more to him than he did to her, he had known that from the beginning. But he would never doubt that in time he would've won her completely over, like he would've Suzy Young and Michelle Benson, and like he did Jenny, before he lost her.

A chill gripped him as the wind gusted, but he was cheered when he recalled the copy of his short story—the Camden version, before Vernon's edits—buried deep in Vernon's archives. He hoped someone far into the future would stumble upon it and marvel at reading the thoughts and true feelings of someone who had lived a long time ago.

A black Cadillac splashed through the flooded street and Charlie was suddenly troubled by the thought that maybe his wasn't a skill anyone would admire at all. The mechanism he had so heavily relied on through-out his life—his innate ability to box his experiences—occurred to him as an impediment against making connections that might allow for personal growth. Even acknowledging the fact, he understood it academically but not emotionally, which was a worry and a lament. However his recent ex-perience had turned out, any vulnerability had passed and he would always remember it as a time when there was a writer named Vernon Downs, and a girl named Olivia, a summer spent in Vermont and then New York, a road trip across the country. When the astounded future listener asked, he would say that the plan all along was for him and Olivia to move to New York, once Olivia had flown back to London to settle her affairs, tell her family and friends. His misguided adventure would be reduced to a few anecdotes about how he spent his time in New York while he was awaiting Olivia's return.

Over time, the entire episode would even occasion nostalgia.

ACKNOWLEDGMENTS

My thanks to Josephine Bergin, Charles Bock, Christopher Boucher, Rebecca Boyd, Hillary Chute, Brock Clarke, Chris Cooper, Michael Dahlie, Stephanie Duncan, Heather E. Fisher, Mary Granfield, Pete Hausler, Alden Jones, John Laprade, Holly LeCraw, Marianne Leone, Allison Lynn, Stephanie Mabee, Amy MacKinnon, Michael Rosovsky, David Ryan, Ryan Scharer, Whitney Scharer, James Scott, Elizabeth Searle, Elizabeth Solar, Lavinia Spalding, Benjamin Strong, Mary Sullivan, and Eugenio Volpe as well as

The Hotel Bar Book Club

My Arizona family

My New York family

My Boston family

My Bennington family

My *Post Road* family

Dan Pope

Clarkes, Gilkeys, Kaliens, and Cottons

Mary Cotton and Max

Bret

Jaime Clarke is a graduate of the University of Arizona and holds an MFA from Bennington College. He is the author of the previous novel *We're So Famous*; editor of the anthologies *Don't You Forget About Me: Contemporary Writers on the Films of John Hughes*, *Conversations with Jonathan Lethem*, and *Talk Show: On the Couch with Contemporary Writers*; and co-editor of the anthologies *No Near Exit: Writers Select Their Favorite Work from "Post Road" Magazine* (with Mary Cotton) and *Boston Noir 2: The Classics* (with Dennis Lehane and Mary Cotton). He is a founding editor of the literary magazine *Post Road*, now published at Boston College, and co-owner, with his wife, of Newtonville Books, an independent bookstore in Boston.

www.jaimeclarke.com

www.postroadmag.com

www.baumsbazaar.com

www.newtonvillebooks.com